A Trip to The Myakka Cutoff

A Shamus Pickford Story

By

David Earth

David Earth's other titles:

Turtle Bay
Riviera Marina!
By-Catch

This is a work of fiction. All the characters and events portrayed in this book are fictional, and any resemblance to real people or actions is purely coincidental.

Author's Note:

The Shamus Pickford stories are all rooted in Southwest Florida, where I aim to inject culture, the working man/woman struggles, the hardships, and the underbellies of everyday Floridians into my work. At times, I feel I've done them justice.

Florida's rapid growth has made it increasingly difficult for the simple-living waterman to sustain his way of life. That's one of the reasons I felt compelled to write these stories—to preserve in amber the "way it was," as vital to our cultural memory as plankton is to an oyster. With so much of Florida's past being swallowed up and paved over, the responsibility of remembering what once was now falls to longtime locals and storytellers.

These stories were written in the quiet hours—on days off, in stolen moments of spare time. The locations described throughout these books, and in most of my salt-soaked work, are real places, or at least, they were when the stories first took shape. As I write this, some of those very spots stand on the brink of erasure, threatened by the steady march of development. Bearing witness to this transformation provides a constant, if bittersweet, source of inspiration.

Year after year people flock to Florida, in specifics the Southwest coast, where it's dodged the dozers longer than the east coast. But as of late, it seems Pandora's box has finally been open. Huge corporations have, over time, weaseled their way into the community, funded many different programs to the unwitting recipients, only to come collect in the way of environmental destruction.

This note is by no means a call to protest. Growth is a force that cannot be stopped but must be done with the environment a top concern.

The short Shamus Pickford books can be on the technical side, some confusing lingo, or mentions of a strange location, that may only be familiar to the locals, who have lived in the areas described. It was not intentionally written that way.

Getting these stories "out there" has been an arduous process with many setbacks. It's hard to say whether I'd continue these past three or four.

The first blip of Shamus Pickford and his associates came to me when a friend and I were casting lures at a dock in a private basin on the east coast of Charlotte Harbor in the early 2000s (nearly 20 years before its first publication). I came to understand it from the bow of my skiff, watching the land flatten beneath the teeth of machines, as hulking new structures rose faster than the eye could blink. The basin described in these pages is real—still there, still fished, still breathing—but like so much of old Florida, its days may be numbered. The model for Shamus's house with the boat ramp was there at one point, only to have been torn down, and in its place a monstrosity of a house built overtop the ruins. Growth is growth.

It was sad to see it go, and I tried to remember it the best I could. I'd spent a lot of time fishing in that basin and along those docks, that I felt the need to preserve its memory, or at least a vague motif.

These books are not perfect. They aren't massive works of literature either, but I hope they capture interest, if only for a moment. When it was time to sit down and finally hash these things out, I did a good portion out on my skiff. The rough drafts lived nomadically in my head for years and prying them out clearly, and onto paper, was no easy task.

They were written mostly outdoors, which is where I choose to write the majority of my stories—it's where the muse is the strongest. Outdoors can be extremely inspirational. For me, a fine view and a cup of coffee is motivation at its best. I've had an on-again off-again relationship with this series over many years before struggling to their final drafts. I honestly thought I'd never finish them, but here we are.

*"The individual has always had to struggle
to keep from being overwhelmed by the tribe.
If you try it, you will be lonely often,
and sometimes frightened.
But no price is too high to pay for the privilege of
owning yourself."*
-Friedrich Nietzsche

*"A man thinking or working is always alone,
let him be where he will."*
*"I never found the companion that was so
companionable as solitude."*
*"To be in company, even with the best,
is soon worrisome and dissipating."*
*"Solitude is not measured by the miles of space between
a man and his fellows."*
-Henry David Thoreau
(Walden; Or Life in the Woods)

"The aim of life was meat. Life itself was meat. Life lived on life. There were the eaters and the eaten. The law was: EAT OR BE EATEN. He did not formulate the law in clear, set term and moralize about it. He did not even think the law; he merely lived the law without thinking about it."
-Jack London (White Fang)

"All water had a perfect memory and is forever trying to get back to where it was.
-Toni Morrison

A Trip to
The Myakka Cutoff

Chapter One

Initially, the charter began flawless—bait, weather, and a solid bite came together in perfect sequence. The three women, who'd booked a "girl day" charter, couldn't have made the day more pleasant. They were hooking fish, trading pleasantries, talking about their husbands, even sharing the unexpected thrill of stepping into their fifties.

After I taught one of the women a helpful technique to bait her hook, and a specific casting technique conducive to live bait, she shared the information, and soon, all three ladies were basically on autopilot. So, as they baited their own hooks and cast themselves, I sat back and marveled at what a pleasant day it was.

"Amazing," I mumbled while taking in the cloudless and storm-free horizon. "My job just became a lot easier."

My head turned when the baitwell pump kicked on, sending shadows of greenbacks swirling like a bowl of sardine soup. I'd anchored us along the eastern wall of Charlotte Harbor and had the ladies tossing live bait lines at a submerged oyster bed—a spot that had been marinating in the back of my mind for months, and today was the right time to indulge. As a cool breeze swept across the water, it produced a one-inch-high surface ripple, just high enough to blur our presence and keep the fish biting.

This area generates exceptional fishing during a fast, outgoing tide because currents washing overtop the exposed oyster bed create an audio effervescence that I believe turned on the bite. Certain species have learned that this water surge might loosen, and in turn, flush out a variety of coverage-depending creatures, which meant food to an awaiting predator.

All three woman were grouped on the bow, speaking in the same Wisconsin accent, and in their early fifties, couldn't have been more entertained. Every mullet that flung itself from the water, the tall woman shouted, "Oh my! See that fishy jump?"

The other two responded in sync: "Yes, Gina…" Gina was wearing a spring hat with a pink bow tied around the crown. Her wet Capri pants soaked through and clung tightly to her full figure.

Suddenly, Gina hooked a nice fish, but before she could put a handle on it, the line tugged the rod from her weakening grip.

"Crap," I said—was rather comfortable sitting in my captain's chair.

Gina's head swiveled toward me faster than the rod flung from her grip and into the water. "Oh, no! I'm so sorry, I didn't mean—"

My eye locked onto the fishing rod as the fish towed it away from the boat. No time to think, I had to retrieve it, so I dipped into the water, a time-acquired reflex. "Well, this spot is ruined for the remainder of the trip…" I mumbled.

"What's that dear?"

"Nothing, Gina," I said using an unambiguous edge in my tone. "It's okay."

As I slogged through waist-high water, a flicker of rosewood-colored light from the darting fish determined its species.

Each woman tried their best to pinpoint the rod.

"Right there, buddy!" one of them shouted.

"Over there!" said another.

My rod appeared lodged two feet deep, wedged into a semi-submerged sharp batch of oysters. I stretched for it, only to have it pull from my reach. Mr. Redfish was still hooked. The women noticed.

"Oh my God!" Gina said. "It's still on."

I kept an eye on the rod, fought for a step in its direction, then snatched it, lifting it from the water, only to find the redfish had escaped.

It then came to my attention that I'd waded twenty yards from the vessel, and that the anchor had pulled loose, setting the skiff adrift. I understood that the tide, with its current direction, would drift my skiff toward the damaging oyster bar.

"Figures," I said.

Things went downhill after Gina decided to take things into her own hands and did the unimaginable. At the wheel, she searched for what I assumed was the ignition.

"I got it, hon," she said.

"No, no. It's quite alright," I voiced to her from out twenty yards.

She replied, "Oh, you betcha. I know boats, and for sure this is my fault. I'll just skim us away."

My concern for the safety of my skiff mounted. "Really, please don't. It's okay. I'll get it—" As I ended the sentence, she found the ignition, cranked it over, and placed the engine in gear. "Not good," I mumbled.

She hit the throttle, not realizing she'd turned the engine hard port. It swung the stern starboard, toward a wad of high-rise oysters. I could only watch at this point.

Realizing her careless mistake, she attempted to correct the chaos by reversing the throttle, which dumped heavy waves of water overtop the low transom, filling the bilge. Panicked, but almost in the clear, she levered the boat into forward gear and pressed down on the throttle rod, heading for turmoil.

I placed my free hand on my head. "Wait, the anchor!"

My words went ignored as the anchor dug in, swinging the stern overtop the oyster bar, slicing up the water, and my propeller. Her eyes widened as it hit, and she asked me for advice. I said the first thing that came to mind.

"Turn *it* off … the engine!"

By engine, she must have heard tilt or trim, because she again attempted to correct the soft grounding by using her wits.

The engine's RPMs spiked as the propeller lifted above the water. Gina noticed and decided lowering the engine back into the water was best, cutting into the who-knew-how-old oyster mound, spewing a spiral of water and circular mud.

A ruckus-bothered cormorant, attempting to dry its wings, flew from its perch as chips of shells peppered the mangrove limb.

As my heartrate spiked, Gina finally found the ignition and deadened the engine. I reached the skiff fighting the urge to be impolite.

"Guldarn it. I'm sooo sorry," she said. "I was only trying—"

I swiped up my hand, and in a calm voice, kept the reply short. "It's o-kay."

"No. For sure, I need to fix it," she said. "I'll pay for it real quick, really."

I handed the fishing pole up to the third woman, who shuddered as she placed it into the rod holder.

"Okay, that would be nice of you." I remained calm, and holding the anchor line from the bow, pulled the skiff clear from the scene.

Her friends began ripping Gina a new one. "Uff da, c'mere. What were you thinkin'? You could've ran him over, Gina!"

Gina continued apologizing: "I know! I feel so bad, yah know!"

I hadn't even thought that this woman could have run me over. Now in my head, I saw the headline: *Local Charter Captain Run Over and Chopped in Half by Client.*

"Perfect," I whispered. "It seems the morning's perfectness—the bait, the weather, the good bite—were all too perfect and had been cleverly balanced by unknown forces."

"What's that dear?"

"Oh nothing…"

I sullenly maneuvered my skiff a few feet from the treacherous oyster bed, and

inspected the foot of the sixty-horse-power engine. Passing the beam, muddy water and bits of slashed oyster shells were floating on the surface. I raised the engine using the tilt button mounted on the engine cowling, exposing the propeller. After a few precise spins, I concluded that, other than a few small dings, no major damage had been done. Later today, I'd remove it for inspection to better gauge the possibility of internal damage.

"Looks like everything is fine back here," I whispered to my reflection in the stainless steel, four-bladed propeller.

Gina heard. "Oh, thank God!"

My face was hidden when my eyes rolled. I then spun the propeller one last time while listening for anomalous noises— none.

At the stern, I lifted one leg on a failed attempt to board the skiff. Gina noticed and offered me her hand.

"Oh, please, let me help you."

I leaned away, heading for the transom. "It's fine, I've got it."

One of them said, "Oh, believe you me, he can do it—just leave him be, Gina."

Now toward the stern, behind the engine, and still in the water, something caught my eye suspended in oyster chunks and broken shells.

As I swept my hand through the water, I realized it was an unknown object, floating in a mix of hacked-up shells and marl. The women were pre-occupied discussing alternatives to Gina's helping skills and noticed nothing.

It nestled neatly in my palm, the grime slipping away as I rinsed it in the water. I gave my hand a quick shake and lifted it to the sun, where a tiny artificial fish caught the light. After peeking at the ladies, I stuffed it under my fishing shirt and sloshed back to the bow of the boat.

Chapter Two

After dropping the three Wisconsin ladies at the Ponce de Leon Park boat ramp, and it being storm season, I had limited dry air and headed home fast and skinny. Thanks to Gina's drawn-out apology, I'd lost some precious dry time and had to rush, but if her tip said anything, it was: what accident?

At the entrance to my basin, Spinner, the local dolphin, laid down a triumphant tail-slapping welcome, then rode tight on portside. I'd noticed for the last six months the dolphin hadn't ventured far from the quaintness and safety that the basin provided. Lately, it had taken to spending most of its time here, where plump mullet were plentiful and easy to harass.

I passed my friend Flip's manufactured house. Hundreds of crab traps, lined up, row after row filled most of the backyard. Normally, Flip was out harvesting mullet, but it appeared he'd switched to crab. "Business must be slow," I mumbled. Tied next to his twenty-four-foot Sheffield sat the old Carolina Skiff that he'd set to retire on cement blocks. Yours truly scraped the bottom barnacle free. Although I still owned my dive tanks, that business had puttered down since I'd switched focus to my guiding services.

I'd been in the guide business now for eleven years and counting—license free. Not saddled by arduous rules was an advantage to me. Around every corner, Florida officials try to tack on another permit, or another restriction. The amount of regulations, and the cost of pricey permits would make it difficult for me to produce a decent living, so I bypass all the red tape.

Immediately after high school, I figured I needed to do something with my life. Spending time out on the water was the only way I felt free. Free from the burdens of land life. So, the decision to become a charter guide came easily.

Pulling up to the house, I moored to my houseboat, which was coincidently this weekend's entertainment. For the past few months, I'd been on a hard course to update things on the old twenty-four-foot pontoon. I'd added a front casting deck and rescreened all the windows. The most important improvement was re-powering the old Johnson one-hundred and fifteen horsepower engine to a newer four-stroke.

After a tug test on the dock line, satisfied my figure-eight double-hitch cleat knot would hold, I proceeded up toward the house. My one-and-a-half-year-old overzealous cur dog named Scupper greeted me with her usual butt wiggle.

She seemed diehard on wagging herself to death, so I found the pet life preserver and clipped it around her body. Her keenness to the fact that when I reached for it, it seemed to be playtime—and I didn't mean with me—was a sample of her intelligence. She'd made a remarkable friendship with the resident dolphin. The two of them seemed to enjoy each other's company, so who was I to change it?

Before I could get the straps tight, she pulled free from my grasp, ran off in a joyful woof, sprinted toward the dock, barking, sniffing the air, yearning to find the gray mammal. Out of a natural instinct to protect, I gazed toward the mouth of the basin. In the distance, white clouds were bubbling up and morphing into gray thunderheads. As the winds hailed from the southwest, the probability that an ominous rainmaker would arrive before dinner time grew with every passing day. I decided Scupper could handle herself and entered the house to perform one simple task: brew a fresh cup of coffee. The beans were fresh and had arrived recently, sent by my good friend Robert Dean. He'd purchased the beans in bulk from a distributor in Texas, who imported them from Mexico. After dripping a full cup, I removed my shirt and found the fish trinket where I'd tucked it, then marveled once again at its unique form. It resembled no modern piece I'd ever seen. Its base had a hole through it, and some manner of string or rope threaded through a tiny hole—perhaps to hang from the neck.

I twisted on a lamp next to a door mirror in the corner of the room and examined it closer. At the head of the fish figurine, two pinhead-sized, shiny green stones gave it eyes. It had tiny gills slits outlined in black that entered a hollow body. Sand and bits of shell filled the hollowness, and taking a quick, deep breath, I removed them using a concise blast of air. Grains shot through the fish's gill holes while the shell particles remained. A local visitor shop could've been crafting these figurines for years, selling them as a novelty item to gullible tourists, but it also might be in some way valuable. It was a wonderful find, so I placed it down my pocket. Then I thought with the coming total eclipse, and the found trinket, what a strange coincidence.

I exited the room toward the garage, gathering a few needed items for this weekend's excursion. My friend Robert Dean was flying in from Asheville for a long weekend of beer, boats, and sunburns. The eclipse was a bonus. Even though they're predicted thousands of years in advance, neither one of us had known about it until last week.

Every few years I plan an escape to rinse the static from my head, a break from the churn of mainstream noise. It works, because out there on the water, stripped of clutter, I can reflect, measure the distance between what I'm told and what I know. Whether it's the blue of the sea or the green canopy of the beautiful mangrove bush, each trip grants a chance to relearn, to uncover small truths. And if nothing else, it reminds me that meaning, however fragile, is ours to find within.

Outside, I found my oversized cooler and emptied it of the useless odds and ends. Provisions would be limited because survival at the bare minimum was part of the plan. After stuffing the cooler with all the usable gear I could find—adding eating utensils, cans of beans, limited rain gear, and an old bottle of Maker's Mark—my phone signaled a message.

It was from Sara: *Need anything?*

She was on her way to the house.

I replied: *Just you.*

Sara Albright and I's echelon of relationship seriousness had inevitably increased over time. Her unwillingness to label us was one of her most attractive qualities. "Let's just be *us*," she always said, adding, "Putting labels on relationships is people's way of understanding where they stand emotionally. But for us, hon, it's unnecessary. Our actions tell us where we stand, Shamus!"

We met after I replied to an online ad for my Toyota. Sara was there during the negotiations—Jim Albright's daughter, sharp-eyed and silent while her father and I talked numbers. When the deal was done, he disappeared with my enclosed trailer. I left with the truck … and his daughter.

She'd been looking for a side hustle. I happened to have one. That's how it started—not romantic, not at first. For a time, we worked side by side, scraping barnacles from hulls in the hot, salt-heavy air. The sight of Sara fitting into a yellow wetsuit; her vibrant blonde hair, high rise cheeks, and clear blue eyes was the image I wanted burned deep into my long-term memory.

*****

If everything went as planned, tomorrow morning my good friend Robert Dean and I would depart from my private saltwater basin and embark outward to the unknowns of Charlotte Harbor. The most exciting part about the vacation was that we didn't have a plan, just take a few days and regroup, "recharge the batteries" some might say. I'd lived most of my life on the water, but my friend wasn't so lucky.

After topping the Coleman off, I loaded it into an aluminum yard cart and made for the dock. As I approached, there were zero signs of Scupper. I called to her before I reached the wobbly plank connecting the dock to the seawall. After I lowered the cooler from the cart, faced up toward the house, I called again—still no sign of her. "Hmmm." I thought that was interesting, so I walked the plank, climbed onto the houseboat's roof, and searched toward the small shoal that marked the beginning of the basin. "Old reliable," I said.

Standing on all fours wagging her tail, Scupper was facing the blackness of the water. Yet again, she'd swam to the shoal at the mouth of the basin in hot pursuit of her friend Spinner. Then, twenty feet off the shoal's edge, the water broke with sudden violence. The dolphin seemed to be thrashing in an aggressive manner toward the pup, echoing hard tail slaps across the water. I wasn't a pet whisperer, but I sensed the pup's reluctance to swim back.

I called out to her, "Here, girl … it's okay!"

Scupper's ears perked, and she sniffed the air. Her foreleg pawed toward the water but snapped back. Just as a second paw dipped, the dolphin blocked her entry, producing spiraling surface boils, circling, stirring the light water immediately ahead of the pup.

I blocked the sun with my palm. "What's going on here?" I mumbled as I focused. "At least the life jacket is still holding."

Spinner's erratic behavior began to harsh my vibe, so I left the roof of the houseboat, untied my skiff, and made toward the disturbance.

On approach to the shoal, Scupper's vocals began to increase to a fluctuating whine. Spinner then surfaced aggressively. Not quite a warning, but far from its usual greeting. It eyeballed me as it surfaced once more and swam off by means of a boat-listing tail thrust, forming a massive boil abreast of the skiff. "Is she warning me?" Once I reached the shoal, it was clear the mammal had marooned Scupper. Scupper needed no encouragement once the bow became soft-beached and leaped onto the deck of the skiff, shook dry, rattling the straps of the pet life preserver.

As I puttered away, Spinner surfaced again and let out a *poooeeeesh* close enough to glaze me in a light sheet of salt-mist blowback. I muttered, "Has this thing gone mad?"

Approaching my neighbor Flip's dock, Scupper's whine morphed into a yelp, slapping her tail the white bow deck. "Good girl."

Puttering past my neighbor, I noticed Flip's yard had been neatened up to some degree. Most of the crab pots were aligned and stacked, and the house's white vinyl siding appeared to have been scrubbed clean, leaving small circular brushstrokes.

Up ahead, Sara was the subject of Scupper's attention. She stood on the dock, a hand blocking the setting sun. White strings from her cut jeans tangled her thighs. The white, skintight T-shirt paired well with her green flops and tanned-even feet. A toe ring caught a beam of light and reflected. Scupper's whole body twisted in excitement.

"Hey, baby," she said.

"Hey," I responded.

"I was talking to Scupper." Sara grinned, focusing on the dog. "What's the matter ... how come she couldn't swim back?"

Before answering, I wondered if I should conceal the real reason, which was Spinner's odd behavior. When Scupper first began swimming in the small basin, Sara, from day one, had been skeptical of the dolphin's intentions.

I met her halfway. "I'm not sure. She didn't want to swim back so I picked her up."

Sara scanned the water out toward the shoal. I speculated that her actions were those of a protective parent or, most likely, trying to find a hole in my story.

Things were going well with us as of late. The foundation of our relationship seemed to be a certain type of humor. Relationship humor was just as important as other aspects, and psychologically rewarding, and we'd found it.

After lashing the skiff to the houseboat, and Scupper between us, I met Sara on the rickety pine dock. The scent of fresh laundry caught my attention.

Sara stole a few cat-like steps onto the plank separating the dock from solid ground, checking for a shudder. The dock was in better condition than a few months ago. Even with the slow pace of repairs, I'd made stability a priority, replacing the injury-prone rotted planks with new composite plastic ones.

After balancing, Sara took the first cautious steps, then leaped onto the soft patch of sugar sand, mumbling, "You need to fix this … jeez."

I centered the plank before I crossed. Scupper trotted across with nothing but ease.

While we hit the light trail leading up to the house, I asked in a high-pitched voice, "So sweetie, what do you want for dinner?"

Sara smiled. "Oh, are you cooking *me* dinner tonight?"

I felt down, using my hand, and tried to find the dog's head. "I was talking to Scupper."

In her expression, I could tell she wanted to say *touché*, but instead led me away using her eyes, slapping me so hard on the ass that even the dog jumped back.

"Oh, you think you're funny?" I said, then chased her the full way up to the house, catching her only as she stopped to open the lanai door.

She lifted her head. "What time are you leaving tomorrow?"

"First thing."

"First thing? What does that mean?"

"It means early," I answered.

"Early?" she said, shaking her head. "Shamus, early for you is ten o'clock in the morning. For everyone else it's dawn."

"Okay, then … between dawn and ten a.m."

Scupper left us and rounded the corner, plopping down next to the doghouse I'd built her.

Sara's eyes pinned on Scupper. "Why is it she never goes *in* the doghouse? She just lies outside it, like sitting on a doggie porch."

I peeked from my sitting position. "I'm not really sure. Maybe she doesn't like it?"

Sara brushed my reply off as though I'd never said it and joined me inside the lanai at a small card table. She sat across from me, picking a hangnail on her thumb. A brief wave of awkwardness clouded our vibe.

"Is everything okay?" I asked.

"How long will you be gone?" she asked.

"Um … just a couple days. Should be back Sunday evening. I've booked a charter Monday, so…"

"Oh…" she replied.

I could hear the dryness in her voice. I'm no expert, but I wasn't sure she understood what the trip was all about, so I began to man-explain. "I'll only be gone a few days. It's a guy weekend. You know, get out and explore new lands … no big deal."

"I know, but—"

"Hey, at least we aren't going to Vegas."

"Funny…" she replied soft and quick. "Isn't there a solar eclipse this weekend?"

"Yes, there is."

"I thought we could watch it together?"

These were tough questions from Sara. I'd love nothing more than to have a romantic afternoon with her, post outside atop the houseboat, and watch the event.

I grinned. "You'll be the only one my mind will know when the sun goes black."

She blushed hard. "Promise?"

"I do, yes. Listen, every so often guys need a weekend away, to do guy things … it's really no big deal."

Her hope was rising. "Well, how come he can't invite his wife and we make it a couple's thing?"

"We can do that sometime, sure, but we've been doing these trips for more than a decade now. It's important. The whole reason for his departure is to get away from his…" I paused and thought of a tactful way to explain myself. Settled with, "Take a break from his mountain life."

The reaction on her face proved my heedful delivery had failed.

"What?" she asked. "You mean to get away from his wife?"

"No, it's not like—"

"Is that what *you're* doing? Getting away from me?" She trailed off. I had to swoop, plug the hole in her emotional dam.

"No—I didn't mean it like that."

"It sure sounded like that, Shamus."

I'd been wondering, after dating Sara for several months, if this side of her existed. Up until now she'd been understanding of the inner-workings, and simplistic nature of my psyche.

"What I meant is, it's just a break from the monotony of everyday life … wife, kids, job … all those things."

Her reaction suggested every time my mouth opened, I receded back two steps. I switched to damage control and slid the plastic chair in at her side.

"The monotony of everyday life?" she said. "Well, I'm sorry your life is *so* monotonous."

I turned her head to face me. "Listen for a minute?"

She faced away with a pouty lip.

"You know I'm not trying to get *away* from you … c'mon now, that's ridiculous."

"Is it?"

"Yeah, it kinda is. Becoming upset at this is like getting upset at every single person who's ever taken a vacation. That's what vacation is … a break from work. In fact, I think it's the actual definition, or close to it."

"A break from work? So, I'm work?" That didn't help. Her face suggested I'd wounded her, a leg kicked out from the table that held our relationship up.

I slipped in and gripped her narrow shoulders. "Listen…" I pointed at her, then back at me. "This … this is okay. You need not worry about *this*." Again, I pointed. "So, tell me what's *really* bothering you."

She relaxed in my arms, releasing the tension as though spilling a static-filled drink. She sat back and we enjoyed a comfortable moment.

Sara's eyes stayed busy inspecting the tips of her hair. The moment passed and she changed subjects. "Are you taking Scupper?"

My eyebrows rose. "I was hoping you might watch her?"

"I guess…"

"Or I could take her … its fine—"

She cut me off, was now sympathetic. "No, it's *okay*. I'll take her to my parents'."

"Are you sure?"

Sara rose hopeful and tippy-toed to the window facing the doghouse and said, "Yeah, she'll have a blast with my parents' bulldog."

"How old is that dog now?"

After a brief, thoughtful moment, she worked the math out loud. "Well, we've had him since I was fourteen or fifteen so he must be pushin' … seventy in human years."

"Wow, not sure what kind of play pal he'll be for Scupper. That dog," I nodded toward the window, "demands attention."

"Don't you worry," she said. "Chewy can handle himself."

I smiled. "I'm not worried about Chewy. I just don't want Scupper getting bored, you know, not getting the enrichment she deserves."

Sara received my statement as intended and rolled her eyes to my antagonizing banter, and on flat feet, stepped toward the kitchen, adding swing to her hair. In there, she freed two beers from the cooler and handed one to me.

"How'd the charter go this morning?"

"It went pretty good until…"

After explaining what had happened concerning the three Wisconsinite ladies, according to Sara's smile, I appeared to have summoned the world's smallest drop of sympathy. I ran with it and said, "Crazy, huh?"

Sara shook her head. "What a stubborn broad."

"Oh, that reminds me, I want to show you something." I removed the small fish bone relic from my pocket. "Here, check this out." By the cord, I handed Sara the small mysterious trinket.

"You found this out on the water?"

"Yeah."

She held it close to her eyes like a jeweler.

"The propeller unleashed it from a chunk of oysters."

Sara continued to examine the fish, its shape, its size, the material in question. "Is this made from bone, or—?"

"Your guess is as good as mine."

"How old do you think it is?"

"I'm not sure of that either. I'm assuming pretty dang old, though."

She began to examine the cord that allowed the fish to be worn as a necklace. "What kind of string is this stuff?" One hand held the item, and the other held the cord.

"I haven't the foggiest idea," I answered. "I'll have to do some research."

Sara swung the fish around her finger like lanyard car keys and handed it back to me, which was the reminder that I had to pick Robert Dean up at the airport tonight at eight o'clock.

Sara picked up on my intentions as I glanced at my watch. "What time is Robert Dean's plane landing?"

"Eight-ish."

"Well, it's almost six. Don't you think you should get goin'?"

"Yeah."

Sara walked me to the truck. We then said goodbye. There was an awkward pause, a brief intermission of intentions.

I prodded it along. "Are you sure you don't mind taking Scupper?"

She again agreed to take the pup.

Chapter Three

Robert Dean's flight arrived an hour late from the Punta Gorda Airport, and so I spent the time attempting to make sense of my recent find. I thought hard and recalled vaguely reading that the Maori people of New Zealand had carved fishhooks from whale bones, but nothing of substance.

Up in the smokey mountains, my friend Robert Dean's ranch style house sits in the woods on an eighteen-acre homestead. For a profession, he runs his own septic business using the slogan: Your Shit Is My Bread and Butter. Heavy footed, he walks bulky but was a wiry kind of guy with hands that could crush a coconut. My friend's been married three times, but the last one he said was a keeper.

"Ain't there an eclipse this weekend?" Robert Dean asked in the passenger seat.

"Yep, sure is. During the day. Supposed to turn the fish on, like a killer nighttime bite."

He clapped his hands. "Fantastic!"

"I'd like to be ready with some nice live bait right after," I said. "Might be the best bite of the year."

"*I've* got the best bite of the year…" he said, digging for something in his bag.

Robert Dean then faced me and smiled as though he had just found the cure for Erectile Dysfunction, a smile that should have been across a child's face. His candid expression was comical as he pulled a glass container from the bag that looked like a jar of gasoline.

He cracked the lid. "I got what you want right here." He lifted the jar up to his nose and sniffed the fumes.

"Is that what I think it is?" I asked.

"Oh, yeah, sure is." His arm extended, offering me a whiff.

Before I could manage a close, personal sniff, I could already smell the sharp, potent odor. I leaned away, entered my driveway, and rolled to a stop.

"Wow, that's some strong stuff," I said, exiting the truck.

"Sure is, bub, and I tell you what, if you need a little t'clean the rust stains off your skiff, it'll do that too." He let out a high-pitched laugh that echoed throughout the yard. "Good ol' apple pie!" he added.

Outside, the air was dead, stagnant, every word sounded crispy, as though it came from miles away.

We walked the concrete path leading to the house. Robert Dean noticed the car cocoon parked next to Scupper's doghouse.

"Is that the ol' Wrangler?"

"Sure is. She's almost roadworthy again."

"Perfect!"

"Well, assuming the road isn't too picky."

Even in the pitch dark, my friend strode to the jeep and lifted a patch of blue tarp next to the front bumper, spilling a handful of collected rain.

He patted it like a dog. "There she is. I remember all the good times we had in this here ol' girl."

I walked up to him. "Yeah, she's been under construction for a while."

He had one eyebrow raised. "You wanna sell her?"

"Now, you know I can't do that," I responded. "She'll be running before you know it."

He let go of the edge and the tarp flapped down. "Well, you give me first pick at her if you decide to sell her, that's all I ask."

I said, "*You* know I'd rather keep her in the family before letting some stranger put his paws all over her."

"Yee-up, I do."

We both shared a profound laugh and moved inside.

Nostalgia filled the rest of the night. Robert Dean was a few years older than I, and while in high school, he had an uncle who lived down the street from me that he visited every summer. One day, on a two-stroke dirt bike, he came buzzing down the street and asked me if I knew where the gnarly trails were. It just so happened that I did. Been friends ever since.

*****

The next morning. I dressed in a fresh, gray-hooded fishing shirt, black boardshirts, fitted a white visor atop my head, and went out the door to the kitchen, then remembered not to forget my new lucky charm—the fish necklace.

Robert Dean swept into the room.

"How'd you sleep?" I asked as I poured coffee.

"Like a baby."

My friend's attire was as comical as his accent. He'd dressed in jean-suspenders covering a white T-shirt along with a mild five o'clock shadow. His white trucker's hat had the word GLOCK stitched on the cap. Underneath the cap, dark brown hair hung longer in the back than in the front, which overlaid his ears.

"Couch okay for you?"

"No complaints here."

"Figured it'd be no problem for you. If your bed lay on a runway at Tampa International, you wouldn't miss a second of shuteye." I then asked, "Coffee?"

"Oh, that reminds me." He raced into the family room, returned less than a minute later holding a red-lettered brown bag of coffee.

I began pouring a second thermos of coffee. "Coffee?" I repeated.

"Well, I didn't bring this bag here…" He shook the coffee beans. "…to watch *you* drink some."

"I haven't finished the last bag yet. You still takin' it blonde?"

"Blonde?" he scoffed. "What are you talkin' about?"

"You know … thick cream. Maybe some vanilla or caramel?"

His expression was sharp, penetrating. "You just leave all the vanilla and caramel for your little girlfriend, you hear?"

"Are you sure? Because I can—"

He snatched the thermos from my hand and sipped. "Ahhh."

"Good?"

He responded with a raised chin. "I like my coffee like I like my yearly financial statement—black, thank you very much."

Out at the garage, I went through a mental checklist. Robert Dean's idea of preparing for a trip was making sure he had a loaded gun and a filled beer cooler. We started off by loading the rods and tackle.

As if preaching fatherly advice, my friend said, "Now, don't you go and forget to bring plenty of chum."

"Check," I said.

"What about the fillet knife? You got one of 'em?"

I held up two fingers. "Check, check."

He continued rummaging through an old box of miscellaneous junk. "Now we're goin' need plenty of bug spray … *with* deet. I remember all the creepy crawlies you dang Floridians got down here. Plus, plenty of toilet paper—"

I held up three fingers. "Check, check, check."

Impressed, he continued searching for something I'd forgotten. But in reality, most of the items had been stowed on the houseboat for quite some time.

I said, "You don't worry about anything, I've got it all covered. Just make sure you bring plenty of ammo in case Jaws attacks the houseboat, okay?"

"Oh, I've got plenty of it back home. I know you don't own a gun, and they ain't allowing them on planes nowadays." He shook his head in a sad realization.

I pointed up to a hook above a small shelf. "Grab the houseboat keys."

"Got 'em," he replied.

As we walked to the dock on the final round of stocking the vessel, my friend asked about the houseboat's maiden voyage that Sara and I took last year. Robert Dean was the one who'd actually paid for the vessel and asked if I'd take her (the houseboat) out on said maiden voyage, in preparation for this very trip. He noticed the new engine.

"Nice."

"You like that?" I asked.

He began playing piano keys on his chest. "Why yes … she-a-quite-a-nice."

"Did you bring the houseboat keys?"

My friend grinned, returning to the garage.

"Watch that first step," I said, referring to the plank. "It's quite technical."

As my friend approached the garage, Scupper began barking maniacally through the lanai door.

"Let Scupper out for me?" I yelled.

He continued stomping forward but flailed his arms: message received.

After a few final checks on the houseboat, I confirmed the skiff's fuel level at half full. I walked back up to the garage, where a tail-wagging Scupper greeted me and fell in at my heels. At the doorway to the garage, Robert Dean was doing some last-minute rummaging.

"You really love junk, don't you?"

"Hey, you be surprised at what people throw away."

I agreed and countered, "But whatever is in that box *isn't* getting thrown away—at least not yet anyway."

Fuel cans in hand, I started to the dock. Robert Dean lagged behind.

Once inside, my friend took obvious pleasure in admiring the twenty-four-foot pontoon houseboat—its teak trim gleaming under a fresh coat of polyurethane. I'd spent hard-earned hours getting the vessel into shape, held to the highest standards, thanks in part to my own admittedly anal-retentive ways. Even the galley got upgrades. I also added additional storage below the main counter and installed a matching stainless-steel sink while a green floral pattern 1970s couch and a fold-out, white plastic card table set in the small living area.

My pride and joy in all the additions was the fifty-five-gallon baitwell installed astern with a low-amp baitwell pump, so it'd run for a week. The before and after photos I'd mailed my friend during the renovation did *not* do the real thing justice.

"Not bad, huh?" I said, marveling.

"Not bad? This looks just as I had pictured it."

"You did picture it. I sent you photos."

"Indeed," he said. "Indeed."

At the wheelhouse, I pointed out a special touch. "How do you like the wheel?"

"Did you?" He blushed. "You didn't...?"

"I did."

Robert Dean admired the custom job I'd done to the steering wheel. Originally, the wheel was just a fraction of a working wheel—dry-rotted cracked plastic. I'd upgraded it to the wheel of an old Bronco II—his first car.

"Where you get this?"

"Thought it would make a nice touch. Got it cheap at a yard sale."

My friend faced me with admiration, gripped the wheel, and spun it a few cold turns.

I added, "I also hope it helps with your pitiful navigation skills."

Robert Dean continued gripping the wheel without acknowledging the jab. "This is just fine ... fine indeed."

"Oh, and check this out." I guided him toward a paper-thin, wood-pocket door and slid it open, revealing the bathroom.

"What's in here? The head?"

"Sure is. It's kinda a cramped space. It's the bathroom minus a shower."

He peeked around. "There ain't no room in here for nothin'."

"Nothin'? Then you can go drop your pants outside with the creepy crawlies."

My friend heard me loud and clear. "Well," he said, reconsidering, "this might work just fine."

With a straightforward toilet—a water tank connected to a saltwater pump. Stomp on the pump three times and it sucked water from below, filling the tank.

After the quick overview of the houseboat, I locked up the house. Scupper was glued to my side as her keen instincts told her I was fixing to leave. I set out a water dish and a new chew toy, which Sara had bought the other day. I noted my watch. The time was 7 a.m.—it was time to depart. I said goodbye and locked Scupper in the house.

We made way, and while passing Flip's house, Spinner surfaced.

Robert Dean observed. "He just follows us all the way out?"

"Now, if he does decide to follow us out, he won't follow us *too* far out."

"Interesting…?"

"It is, as of late, it won't stray far from the basin."

As we vacated my homeport into Charlotte Harbor, skiff in tow, my peripherals caught an offshore flash of heat lightning. The early red sun shone vividly off starboard—its rays split through the dark smear of cloud. Wave slap echoed off the aluminum pontoons as they sliced through the water. Along the East of Charlotte Harbor, down a ten-mile mangrove wall, a familiar sight of far-off splashes signaled groups of lucky pelicans having found breakfast.

Our goal for the next two days was that of relaxation and Zen. The importance of the human psyche to, on occasion, purge itself from the frustrations and uncontrollable factors of everyday life was something I believed in for a long time. The

Charlotte Harbor estuary provided the perfect environment for such reposing motion.

We chugged at a reasonable speed and listened to the pontoon's pacifying rhythmic-like displacing of water. For starters, our destination was Hog Island's southern tip, and as we rounded Whorehouse Point, we passed through a massive school of threadfin herring—a pod comparable to the size of a basketball court, and it wouldn't get overlooked as the water surface trembled like a vibrating puddle. Robert Dean made for the cast net.

I said, "It's in the skiff—back hatch."

Before I finished the sentence, he leapt astern, jerking the skiff close. For a better view, I set the houseboat adrift and climbed up to the roof.

Robert Dean pulled the eleven-foot net from the rear hatch and swung it over his muscle-stacked shoulder; the lead weights settled onto his back.

I asked, "Will you throw from the here or the skiff?"

He answered while inspecting the net. "What you think?"

"I'd say come to the houseboat's bow and we'll run and gun 'em."

Without delay, my friend laid down the net, and using the bow line, tugged the skiff, closing the gap between the two vessels.

I climbed down and took the helm of the houseboat.

At the skiff's bow, my friend pointed to the bait. "Thatta way!"

As fast as a lightning bolt, the bait split up and disappeared below after detecting our sloppy presence. I let off the throttle, settling the engine into a low idle while Robert Dean searched for the right spot.

He was light-footed passing along the gunwale to the houseboat's bow. "Over there?" He pointed using his chin—mouth loaded with lead like a dog jaw-clenching a tennis ball.

In hopes of flanking the pod, I spun the wheel, cutting the boat starboard. My view through the houseboat window wasn't conducive to spotting bait, so I relied on my friend's instructions.

As though with a marble-filled mouth, my friend shouted, "Straighten her out."

Luckily, the pod had resurfaced, and I pointed the bow north.

My friend compressed and readied to launch the net. Just like that, Robert Dean swung, spinning the net north of the bow, opening it like a pancake. I throttled back with a tinge of adrenaline, snatched an empty five-gallon bucket, and met Robert Dean at the bow to lend a hand. Over fifty pieces filled the net, brimming over the bucket—all shimmering and gasping for air.

We wasted no time transferring them to the fifty-gallon stern baitwell, making special effort not to touch a single one. Threadfins have extremely loose scales; even the light touch of a human hand could wipe them loose. The more scales stripped from the bait the more issues we'd have keeping them choke free in the baitwell.

After we poured dozens of white, sun-reflecting baits into the baitwell, my friend reached for the cooler and awarded us with a beer. We each drank a refreshing sip and marveled at our accomplishment.

Robert Dean slurped. "Nothing tickles me more than a full well of white bait."

Unable to come up with a better way of putting it, I said, "Cheers," and held out the can.

"Cheers, bub," he replied.

Our cans clinked, and I took to the wheel and pointed us toward Hog Island, which sat at a precise two nautical miles away.

*****

"How's business?" I asked a short time later.

My friend remained next to me as I piloted the boat toward our destination. "Oh, it's just fine at the moment." His suspenders had a bunch of glitter-like scales reflecting the bright morning light.

"Good, I'm glad."

He shook head in disbelief. "Yeah, you wouldn't believe the things people shove down their drains … my *God*."

"Yeah, I bet they don't understand the damage that will do."

"I mean, just last week I was troubleshootin' a standard gravity system." A possible bait pod caught my friend's eye. He focused back and continued. "Anyhow … typical call this time a year, with all the rain and what-have-you … systems are backed up." He rolled his eyes. "So you know … first thing first, I check the outflow filter, okay? Guess what I found blocking the effluent?"

"What?" I asked.

He winked. "Just guess here for a moment. Let's see what yah got."

I thought for a moment as I checked our course. "Umm … I don't know … hair?"

"Close."

"What then?"

"You're halfway there with hair."

"Hmm…"

A flippin' damn ferret!" he said.

"Wait … what?"

Before answering, he pulled two more dripping wet beers from the cooler, cracked both open, and handed one to me. This time he spelled it out slower. "A flip-pin'… damn … ferret."

"How the—?"

He sipped his beer. "These people forgot to tell me that their pet ferret went missing a couple days prior. I mean, how air-brained can some people be?"

"So … did you show them what the problem was?"

"I sure as heck did, Shamus. I pulled out its long, putrid body and laid it on the driveway right next to the car—wet and all."

"You didn't…?"

"I did. It was during a dangerous heat wave, and the driveway was on fire. I thought the poor bastard was gonna start to sizzle!"

"Crazy."

"Then I called out the whole dang family—father, mother, little twin girls, age ten, and boy, eight."

"I can taste it…"

"Well, taste this: the boy sees it, looks at his sister and says, 'I told you he couldn't swim!'"

"No way."

"Way. The girls ran off into the house, probably to puke, who knows. Then the son walks on over to the rotting carcass and starts poking it with a stick. Incredible, I tell yah."

I shook my head.

"Apparently the boy admitted that he shut the lid and flushed the poor bastard down the drain." My friend's voice rose, and he slapped me on the shoulder and finished with, "…while it was gettin' a lap of toilet water."

"Man … you have all the fun."

"Fun? I'll tell you what's fun. Fun is gettin' woken up in the middle of the night for a

service call, only come to find out the reason the septic tank was backed up is because the night before, the homeowner's teenage son flushed a half pound of marijuana down the toilet because his older sis threatened to rat him out."

"Oh, c'mon. Seriously?"

"I'm not putting you on, Shamus. Should have seen it. A Ziplock bag of the most purple crystallized goodness anywhere east of Colorado."

"Wow. Did you bust the kid?"

"Oh no. I told the parents some lame excuse … like typical drain clog stuff." My friend loaded a mischievous grin. "The bag was sealed and still fresh so…"

"You didn't…?"

"Sure did. It took me two dang hours in the middle of the night to fish that clump of goo from their septic tank, so I gave the son a sneaky wink, took it home, and fired one up."

"What did it taste like?"

My friend's fast-approaching laugh was obvious. "Shit."

Chapter Four

harlotte Harbor's northern rim was home to a region called the Myakka Cutoff—a winding maze of creeks and mangrove hedges that offered a hidden slit through the precarious backcountry, linking the Myakka River with Charlotte Harbor and the Peace River. At mean low tide, to most vessels, the water level created a navigational nightmare. At a formidable high tide though, when there was plenty of depth, hidden oyster beds remained silent under the brackish river water.

The soft, four-stroke engine hummed along. And down at the rum-colored water, small blooms of hydrilla drifted in unilateral clumps.

We entered the mouth of the Cutoff at its southern entrance. The first narrow creek snaked off portside, thinning like a blood vessel. The Cutoff's true significance could only be measured from its ability to produce the largest snook Southwest Florida had to offer.

Certain mangroves, particular to the area, have aged in excess of a hundred years. They have lived, died, and now with gradual pressure, torrential winds and rains had battered them down to hollow, white nubs of their previous form. What white limbs that were still standing had been claimed and put to good use. So, all along Charlotte Harbor's mangrove coast, ospreys find that dead trees make perfect nesting grounds.

Robert Dean slipped to the bow and began to scope out the day's first fishing spot.

I placed the engine in neutral and gathered my bearings. Suddenly, the engine began losing water pressure and a high-pitch engine alarm sounded.

Robert Dean heard it and paused before taking the last step to the bow. "She stall out?"

"Seems so.," I said, letting the motor rest momentarily "Weird." Before turning the starter key, I check all gauges, including fuel, which was topped off. "Here we go." I cranked the starter and the motor piped to a strong, blue-smoke idle.

It was good news, and as we glided at idle speed, I inspected the inside wall of mangroves, searching for the right spot to begin the hunt.

Robert Dean signaled with an antsy thumbs up, and feeling we'd reached an area felicitous to our angling needs, my friend tossed the anchor as if lassoing a loose cow. After the fish-scattering splash, I sighed and throttled into reverse—so as not to bump the skiff in tow.

After I'd positioned the houseboat parallel to the mangroves, I reached for a rod in the main cabin. I asked Robert Dean, who was adjusting the anchor rope from the bow, if he'd like a rod loaded with a threadfin.

He replied, "Does a bear shit in the woods and wipe its ass with a white fluffy rabbit?"

I assumed his answer was yes and met him at the bow, but not before bringing two more beers and two lawn chairs.

After hooking the threadfin through the tail, which caused them to swim away, I handed the rod off and my friend cast out, landing the threadfin with a broadside slap. This one acted in accordance and fluttered on the surface, inviting the bite.

I sat leisurely with my friend to my right in a fold-out, blue lawn chair.

"Look at that little guy go," he said.

I added while watching the threadfin flutter on the surface, "He's gonna get taxed."

With clear skies overhead and no hint of a morning storm, the only distraction was the distant hum of a fading outboard. Ahead, the Cutoff stretched flat as an ice rink, the still water mirroring the sky above. Depth held steady at five feet—just enough murk for the concealment we needed.

"So, how are things with the little lady?" my friend asked.

"Good, good. Oh, and that reminds me." I pulled out my phone. "I need to call her."

He smiled. "Oh, you do, do yah?"

"Yeah … to make sure she gets Scupper." That was only part of the reason. The other was to reassure her that when I returned, we'd have *our* time. I dialed the number and after five rings, her voice: **"Hello?"**

"Hey, it's me."

"Oh, hi…" Her voice was soft and sleepy.

"Got the pup?"

"Yup, at the house now," she answered. I detected a yawn.

"Thanks, I do appreciate it."

"You know I don't mind."

"I know, and I'm glad I can count on you."

She received my message as intended, replying, "Yeah, it's going to be fun. I'm taking her to the dog park."

"She'll love that."

"So," she said, bordering on a laugh. "Is Robert Dean enjoying this time away from his wife?"

"He is, yes," I answered.

She chucked. "Okay … well, you two do whatever it is you're doing and call me tomorrow, okay?"

"Will do."

Lately, Sara's goodbyes had suspenseful silences, which fueled my speculation as to what her motivation was. A subtle pause at a crucial moment, an eye slant while in person, an awkward touch, all seemed to be intentional, a vacant moment specifically for me. My gut told me she might want to say she loved me but leaving these intentional windows for me to say it first.

"Okay, talk to you tomorrow," I said.

"Okay—bye now."

I hung up the phone and stuffed it down my pocket.

"Everythin' good with the dog?" Robert Dean asked, holding up the fishing rod pinching his fingertips on the line.

I grinned internally. "Yes, Scupper is at Sara's parent house."

My friend continued, "So, things seem to be goin' pretty dang good with the lady friend?"

"Well," I began, "…it doesn't seem to be going bad, I'll tell you that."

Robert Dean twitched the rod, shocking the bait into a panic—then asked a follow-up. "How long you two been at it now?"

"Just about ten months or so."

My friend began to reel up the bait when the line sprang taut. He vaulted to his feet. "Fish on!" he chirped in strain.

"Keep the line tight!" I said as the fish circled the houseboat.

Robert Dean followed it to starboard as line screamed off the reel. "Hope this line is fresh, bud!"

"Should be plenty strong, just relined it last week." I stood next to my friend, waiting to assist—my guide habits do die hard. The braided line tightened again, and the fish darted out fifty yards. "She's a runner," I said, and raced into the galley, searching for the net—remembered I stowed it on the skiff. "Don't lose her now."

His voice muffled through the cabin that separated us. "Now, don't you worry about that, I'm in control of this fish!"

I dashed stern-side and leaped onto the skiff, landing hard, nearly rolling an ankle. After finding the net, I rushed to his side. For leverage and stability, I spaced my legs to a proper width and prepared to land the mysterious creature. "Get a look at her yet?" I asked.

He faced me, mouth open, lips pulled tight in strain, exposing polished false teeth. "Not yet, she won't let me gain an inch."

Craving to boost the excitement to the next level, I told him, "There's only one fish I know of that can off rip that amount of drag…"

He knew the answer and faced my way. "Cobia!" Robert Dean gripped the corked rod butt and cranked the handle a full turn, but just the drag clicked.

Cobia, commonly caught in Charlotte Harbor, was known to travel in pairs, will strip your line faster than a catfish on a frozen shrimp, and will eat about anything.

Fighting the fish was taking a brutal toll on my friend's arms. I said, "You're not going to pass out on me?"

"Are you kidding me?" he said, pinning the rod butt against his knee, wiping his brow. "I can fight this fish *all* night!"

"If you don't hurry up, I'm going inside to take an hour nap."

He laughed, an ostentatious brag, which I appreciated. "In an hour, I'll have this fish at the bottom of my stomach!"

After another five minutes of solid fight, the fish had weakened. My friend drug it headfirst toward the mouth of the black dip net I'd lowered into the water.

"Looks like she's forty-plus-inches," I said.

"She's all day forty, might even be twenty-five pounds." He led the fish toward me. "What's legal take home?"

"Thirty-three inches."

"She'll eat." Robert Dean's caution then went to the next level. He'd sinned by way of a fisherman's code by planning the meal before landing the fish. He added in a whisper, as though hiding from bad karma: "She's every bit a keeper."

His thinning, frayed leader was my most concern, as at the last moment, I scooped the fish into the net.

My friend placed the rod down and prepared for hook removal, but the hook by itself had freed. "Whoa ... that was close," he said, holding up the dislodged, bent hook.

I reverted to charter logic. "No big deal—happens all the time."

Before it headed to the fillet station, while presenting the cobia up for a picture, my friend grinned though it was a winning lottery check.

A cobia's head resembled that of a catfish, its muscle-loaded body, long and sleek, the fish was scaleless, gray-skinned, dark like a thunderhead. Its white underbelly reminded me of a snow-covered road, and the dorsal fins weren't fins at all but small retractable razor claws, like in the paws of a lion.

"How you thinkin' about cookin' 'em?" my friend now asked freely.

I lowered the camera phone. "I like to cut them to steaks and lay them on the grill."

Robert Dean brought the fish to the stern as though cradling a baby and laid it where I'd mounted a custom-made rocket launcher fillet station. After a crack of another beer, he sharpened both knives—an eight-inch blade and ten-inch blade. As I sat astern, one leg up on the stainless-steel railing, glancing at the mouth of the Cutoff, I thought it odd no other boats were sharing this gift.

To filet, Robert Dean flattened the curly cobia on the fillet station's white cutting board. For easy handling, he readied the fish and wiped off a coat of light slime.

I rose, handed the eight-inch wooden-gripped fillet knife to my friend. "You want the honors?"

He held the fillet knife, conceded, smiled, and offered it back. "I'm good. Go for it."

I countered, "Oooh no, buddy. This is your fish … you traveled quite a ways to catch it. Really, I insist."

He tossed back a final slug of beer. "All right, if you're goin' twist my stinkin' arm." He held the fish like sawing a log of wood and began cutting at a bias. Then glanced my way and noticed the fish necklace.

"Nice necklace, where did you get that old thing?"

After explaining how I acquired it, he told me his thoughts on what the rope material was made from.

"Are you insinuating this is palm fiber?" I asked.

"Yup, palm fiber is really, *really* good for strength."

"No kidding…" I pondered a second. "So, plenty of people use it, huh?" I said to remain hopeful and save some sense of authenticity to my find.

"Sure … maybe hundreds of years ago."

"Hundreds of years?"

"Yup—or unless you're a tree-huggin' hippie."

"C'mon, I'm sure people still use it. I mean, novelty shops might use it to mess with tourists, to keep the illusion real?"

My friend flopped on the table a mighty solid chunk of fish, slid it clear, and commenced slicing. "Think what you want, Shamus, but that, my friend, might be the real thing."

"Real thing?"

He nodded hard. "Yeah, the *real* thing."

"Like, an ancient artifact or something?"

"Um…" Robert Dean paused, "not exactly ancient … but Native American."

"Native American?" I asked. "Like Indians?"

"You got it," he said. "You know this area was run by The Calusa way back when." Then added, "May even be worth a buck or two." He slid the second fillet my way.

I rolled the tiny trinket using my fingertips, eyes pointed down at it, chin resting on my chest. "Interesting…"

Even after the two healthy steaks had been harvested, the cobia could still feed ten more people. After smearing our filets in butter and olive oil, I brought out a stowed camping stove, steadied it on the fillet table, and lit it. When the scent of previously cooked meals caught my attention, the grill was ready to use.

Robert Dean followed my lead and plopped the oily chunks on the grill, setting off a light sizzle, sear, and smoke. After a few minutes, I flipped over both, revealing fresh, black grill marks. In the cabin, I sifted through the overhead cabinet located in the galley and soon returned to the grill carrying a plastic seasoning bottle. After a few quick wrist flicks, I'd covered the cobia evenly in thin, brown dust.

"What we got for seasoning?" my friend asked.

"It's just some *mild* Creole seasoning,"

"Now ... I've never heard of *mild* Creole seasoning ... there's only one kind of Creole seasoning and that's spaa-cy."

"Nothing gets by you," I said, smiling. "There are mild ones, too."

"Did you forget? I'm from the mountains?"

"Yeah, so what does that have to do with anything?" I asked, spreading the seasoning evenly thought the cooking fish.

"It means we know our way 'round a grill, and all about spicy seasoning. Have you ever heard of Da Bomb?" he asked.

"Hot sauce?"

"Yup."

"Made with ghost peppers?"

"That's the one."

I nodded my head in agreement. "I tried it once—know all about its intensity."

"Let me tell you that back in North Carolina, we tricked this oily fool who used to work for me into eating some. He was always gettin' drunk and actin' dim-witted. Deserved it, in my eye."

I led him on. "Okay..."

"Well, what we did was take one tablespoon and hid it under the cheese on a meat lover's pizza."

"Seriously?"

"Heck yeah, I'm serious. One night after work, a few of my workers ordered a pizza and we were all hangin' out drinking beer and what-have-you. Doug calls up slurring his speech, talkin' all kinds of nonsense."

"I see where this is going..."

"Now, let me finish..." my friend told me.

I lifted the fish off the heat and laid it on a paper plate beside the grill. I said, "Okay, go."

"See, my service manager, Miguel, he steps to his truck, reaches into his glovebox and pulls out this bottle of hot sauce." He formed a grin. "Bein' skeptical, I ask for a sample, okay? Miguel dipped a toothpick inside the bottle and handed the toothpick to me. I looked at him and said, 'Is that it?' He laughs at me and says, 'Joost try it, mane.' So I put this tiny toothpick on my tongue, and by God, my tongue burned afterwards for ten minutes. I tell you this is some hot stuff."

He snagged another beer as I twisted off the propane—then continued, "So Miguel and Doug, they don't get along at all. I have to keep them separated—they don't *ever* ride together."

"Why not?"

"Okay, this is why they don't get along—I'll finish the hot sauce in a minute. They both were clearing this old septic tank out one day and Doug was still in trainin' and learnin' the ropes, you know. So, this sweet old lady's septic was backed up bad … it needed to be cleared and quick. Before the two arrived at the job, they went to lunch. Now, in this line of work, using the bathroom is the last thing on your mind." He looked me in the eye. "*Especially* at a customer's house."

"That should be a no-brainer."

He waved off my statement. "So, this guy takes the mother of all craps in this poor old lady's bathroom *before* the clog's been rectified." Robert Dean gulped a large swig of beer, finishing off the can.

I cut in. "This story is putting a bad taste in my mouth."

"Well, listen to this: the bad part about it is that he made good ol' Miguel clean it all up."

"C'mon—you can't be serious," I said. "Why did he *make* Miguel clean it up? I mean how could he *make* him?"

"Ah … well, Doug pulled the ol' sick card. Went back to the truck and laid his ass down—saying he didn't feel right."

"Well, was he … really?"

"That's the big ol' question, but I'll tell you what, Miguel didn't think so. So, Miguel has had it out for Doug for a quite a while, just about all of the five-and-a-half-months he worked with us."

"So, what happened with the hot sauce … did he eat it?"

"He ate it alright. We had just finished all the pizza but left just one slice. While Doug was on his way over, Miguel had said, 'I beet gringo gonna eat dis last slice. He gonna come right 'een here, won't ask permission, and snatch this slice up.' Then Miguel puts one full scoop of this sauce under the cheese and meat, and then spreads it around as if it were marinara sauce—blending it in."

"Man…"

"Yup—so Doug arrives and walks on in and zips toward the pizza, and without askin' grabs up the slice, and in two bites scarfs down the whole thing."

"Unbelievable…"

"It was hard to watch at first, I tell you, but this guy was such a *pain*-in-my-*ass*, he had it comin'."

"I bet."

"Anyhow, he ate the slice so fast he didn't realize what he'd eaten until it was too late. He'd already gone ahead and rubbed his eyes and scratched his scrotum, see. Some dripped on his fingertips, and that was all she wrote. He went runnin' out to the back of the house, stripped down to his skivvies and put the hose down himself. His lips swelled up and his eyes went puffy, and his junk was redder than a bleeding baitfish."

As I heard the story, I had no response, so just shook my head. "Wow."

"Yup—so when I say I know seasoning, I *know* seasoning."

"I guess so," I replied as I separated the cobia steaks on the paper plates and handed one to Robert Dean.

He took it and waited for silverware while I headed back to the galley. I returned holding two forks.

We both ate our pulpy rewards and sipped beers. After we'd consumed the fish, all that remained were the juicy, moist outlines on white paper plates.

The breeze had picked up, and a surprising thundercloud lingering westerly burped out a disparaging growl while the sun, too, had begun plunging to the west, and every passing minute, reddened and dimmed.

My friend disappeared into the cabin.

In the skiff, moored astern, I double-checked the lines and noted that I'd switched on the auto-bilge. I made my way back to the houseboat and came to know Robert Dean had made his way atop the cabin, onto the lookout.

I climbed, and as I unfolded my seat, I noticed the apple pie-filled mason jar had also made its way up. I flopped down.

"Save some for me?" I asked—then un-cracked the top and sipped.

"Easy," my friend said.

"Easy?" I replied, coughing at the strength of the drink—then in a mocking tone: "Let me tell you how it's done in Southwest Florida…"

My friend laughed and snatched the jar. "Sure is an innn-credible view from up here."

"One of the best," I replied.

A moving tide had drifted the houseboat and faced us north. We sat afloat at the Cutoff's southern entrance, and as the light breeze rippled the surface glass, a group of downward-facing seagulls flew overhead, sensed our devoured fillets of cobia.

"Get on—scat!" my friend barked at the birds.

The cobia and apple pie had begun to settle into my stomach. "Time for dessert," I said.

Robert Dean turned. "Oh…?"

I shook out a bag containing cannabis, which I'd procured from my friend Klinger a few days prior. He had no want for relinquishing his last bag, but after I explained the upcoming festivities, he agreed.

I presented the freshly lit cannabis joint to Robert Dean between my thumb and index finger.

His eyes expanded, recognizing the tightly rolled paper, and said, "It's been awhile for me… Well, since the unclogging incident."

After assuring him that the apple pie foundation had been accurately laid, I stated that the outcome of just a small amount would be more than satisfying.

He took the lit cannabis cigarette, brought it to his lips, eyes slanted, and pulled in the smoke, and after his lungs embraced it, exhaled.

"See, not too bad, right?" I reached for the cigarette—took a similar hit. After two rounds the joint was barely there. I extinguished the remaining bit on the white wooden deck and flicked it out to the Cutoff. Said, "There's more under the wheel, in a small compartment."

"Better than that bag of crap I fished out."

After another swift imbibe of apple pie, I leaned back and let the moment catch up. The mangroves seemed to float above the fast-rising tide, and the meandering storm cloud to the south had dissolved into a thin, white blotch. Before heading far into the bush, an inquisitive osprey swooped low to inspect. An interesting gust pressed broadside against the houseboat. The rotation spun the bow, facing us toward the western mangrove wall. She now sat right at twenty feet from trimming the mangroves, where a half-sunken mangrove log protruded from the placid surface.

The next couple of hours were blurred into one brief moment. My good buddy, Robert Dean, had now worked his way to the houseboat's bow, where he immersed himself in a strident battle with a rather large snook. The fish eluded multiple attempts at capture, breaking off after a brief fight with my friend—a taste test, perhaps a bite-check forewarning his arms to reserve blood and conserve strength, because against this fish he'd need it. He threw threadfins, time after time, tempting the fish to remain in the area and bite again. But time after time he was only given a taste—and left in defeat. But knowing my friend as I did, he would resume.

From above, I shouted, "Try tail-hooking him."

"I've been fishing since I was two years old. I know what I'm doin'." He leaned forward to set the hook yet again.

I wisely believed that the fish might have been privy to my friend's intentions, for it gulped down each chummed bait thrown and deferred the blood-clotted hooked bait.

After not too long, the sun had lowered, and the Myakka Cutoff spun into darkness. A few miles away the nearest ambient light came from the Punta Gorda Bridge.

Thirty minutes later, after multiple casts, Robert Dean succumbed to the apple pie and stumbled onto the vintage sitting couch—rocking the boat.

"Better luck next time," I called down to him.

"I'll get you again, trust me," he mumbled, not speaking to me but out to the pitiless snook.

I stayed above the wheelhouse, perched on the lookout deck, watching and listening as the moonlight stirred the Cutoff to life. Somewhere out there, mullet splashed, their echoes murmuring across the still water. Birds cried out from the fringes—sharp, urgent warnings, likely defensive, guarding nests full of eggs. Maybe a gator was on the prowl. Alligators weren't a common sight in the Cutoff, but from time to time one would slipped down from up The Myakka River to nest in the private, bountiful mangroves.

As the anything but silent night went on, the air became light, easy to breathe, crisp, like early morning fog. Brilliant stars illuminated the mysterious dome above; an occasional meteor shot across the vastness of nighttime.

My arms and legs were stretched, spread out while sitting on a beach chair. I removed my white visor, ran my hands through my long-knotted hair and scratched at the dried sweat. Sitting next to me was the half-filled mason jar of apple pie. I reached for it, popped the top, drank a nightcap, replaced the lid, and set it down. I swatted at the unsympathetic no-see-ums that attack at night. I then gripped my *Buff*, covered my face, and glanced up. Stars had begun spinning around as if I were on a merry-go-round, so I planted a foot flat in hopes of temporarily slowing down the ride.

Disorientation caused me to try standing but instead, I stumbled to the sharp edge of the lookout atop the houseboat. I abandoned the idea after multiple attempts and leaned over, gripped the lip, and peered down to the deck. The water was a few feet out from the gunwale. My stomach tightened, and I braced for what was to come. Without another second of wonder, my stomach contents were now located on the metal taffrail (eight feet down) that surrounded the pontoon deck. I finally rolled onto my back, drifting in that fragile space between waking and sleep, where the apple pie tugged relentlessly at my dimming consciousness, sending me into a pleasant slumber.

Chapter Five

"What in the hell is that? Did you puke all down the railing? Dang, Shamus!"

My friend's voice came at the break of dawn. Its jolt seemed to lance into the center of my brain, like connecting both terminals of a car battery to my ears. I lifted my head and paused. The spins, at first, seemed to have slowed, so I attempted additional movement. The night before had left me lying on the rim of the lookout, resting my head on the ledge, so when I awoke harboring a sharp neck crick, I wasn't surprised. Down below, my friend was dipping a white painter's bucket into the water, using it to clean the vomit off the railing.

"You missed a spot," I called down.

"You missed the water by six inches. I mean, you couldn't move six more flippin' inches?"

"Have you seen where I've slept?"

He didn't look up. "And…?"

"I wasn't able to climb down, dang. You should be thanking me I didn't come down and let it loose on your couch."

"Oh?" He bowed. "Then let me take a minute and give thanks to the all-mighty Shamus Pickford."

I grinned. "You better be." I needed to find equilibrium before trying to descend the eight-foot ladder. After a test step, I nailed down my footing.

Robert Dean commented, "Be careful, now."

I made it down without incident and asked my friend what we were having for breakfast. "I was goin' ask you the same thing," he said.

For a quick rise, I asked, "You want a banana?"

"Banana? Are yah out of your mind? Yah aren't supposed to bring ban—"

My hand was up. "I know, just making sure *you* know." My favorite one is about the banana oil…"

"Oh yeah?"

"Rubs off onto the hands. Spooks the fish."

"That's just ridiculous," he said, swiping his hand at my words. "C'mon, Shamus."

"So, what do you think? Let's hear it, then."

He turned, planted his feet flat. "Everyone knows it's because of the creepy crawly termite."

"Termite?"

"Sure is," he explained. "In Africa, there's a banana eatin' termite. So, imagine draggin' all those bundles across the land, and those little pests latch on, and those bundles load onto a wooden boat? Big trouble…"

"Interesting. Or what about the spider theory?"

He cringed. "More bugs…"

"Yeah, for some reason, spiders love bananas. Imagine crossing the ocean on a ship infested with spiders?"

He shivered and said, "Enough talk 'bout creepy crawlies, okay?" He expressed a razor-sharp cringe and sauntered into the cabin mumbling something obscure.

Pertaining to boats and omens, bananas were as bad as they come. Bringing one aboard under a uniformed captain could get the banana—and you—tossed overboard.

Inside, he found a stash of mangos and grapefruit but didn't look satisfied.

"You don't like fruit?" I asked.

"I can't eat this for breakfast." He air-chewed with his jaws. "I need some sort of meat."

I faced him. "Okay, coming right up." I sifted through the cooler and pulled out a can of skinless and boneless sardines in olive oil.

"Are you kidding me?"

"You said meat. Here's meat, no?"

"I didn't say fish," he answered.

"Well, fish is meat, right?"

"For breakfast? Sardines?"

"They're great with hot sauce." I searched more and managed a can of beans, held it up.

My friend gagged.

"Okay, no beans. It's either that or cobia…"

"Unbelievable." My friend turned down to the cooler, muttering.

"Um, I may have some protein bars here somewhere," I said, thinking about the cabinet to the left of the sink. "Maybe some beef jerky too." I found an old box of breakfast bars, part of the maiden voyage with Sara. "Here's a choco-peanut protein bar." I held the bar out under my eyes, attempting to focus on the microscopic label.

"I'll take it." My friend snatched it from my hands.

"Forgot I had those…"

"Anything is better than fish and beans for breakfast!"

"What happened to 'eat fish all weekend?'"

He snorted and jeered. "Indeed, but not breakfast, c'mon."

I held the box of breakfast bars. "Not sure how fresh they are though. They've been stowed for a long time. Bought them the first time Sara and I took her out for the maiden. Probably have been melted throughout the summer."

He completed a test bite, pausing while his taste buds analyzed the tang of ingredients, afterward sending the findings to his brain for calculation. After a swift few seconds, the results were in, and he proceeded to chew.

"Okay?" I asked.

"It'll do."

"Good," I said, counting the remaining bars.

He saw me placing the box back into the cupboard. "What—no breakfast for you?

"I don't eat breakfast."

As I checked the bait, my friend prepared the skiff for the day's fishing. Dark shadows swam in the churning water inside the oversized baitwell—the bait had survived the night.

We loaded the sticks, and after the baitfish were transferred to the skiff, we de-moored from the houseboat and made way north, toward The Cutoff's backcountry.

A sense of renaissance came with this new day's morning. My activities the previous night had made hydrating a number one priority, so while cruising past mangrove root after mangrove root, above rum-colored water, I drank short swigs from a lukewarm bottle of water.

With our loaded baitwell, we didn't need to scout for bait, and I pointed the bow toward a narrow creek winding off the main Cutoff artery. Specifically, this creek was an old charter spot of mine that, in gradual steps, had returned to its old ways, and began to produce fish again.

As we touched on the mouth, starboard, atop a dead mangrove tree, an osprey had built its nest. It had been months since I'd visited this area, but the nest appeared to have been there for longer than that.

My sight slipped down to the water's surface, where two distinctly, unprofessional pilings had been installed. Fissures, gaps, and haphazardly cut-off branches were visible from all its two feet of exposed trunk. They were pressed-in about twenty feet from an outcrop of mangroves. These waters were at constant risk of modification at any moment, so I didn't think more of it.

I set the engine to idle, and we glided off plane. But a tick past the mouth, a sharp, blind corner required a safety-first approach. We acted guarded when entering the creek, and once the coast was clear, I hammered the throttle and lifted the skiff on plane. The next few switchbacks opened to a vast improvement in visibility. As we skimmed along on the greasy flat water, overgrown mangroves appeared that I hadn't noticed before. While gliding ten feet off the mangroves on a hundred-yard straightaway, we finally rounded the corner ahead of the intended target when the skiff slowed abruptly, like driving into a giant rubber band. The engine wound up, redlined, and therefore stalled, sending Robert Dean head-first onto the bow. I was lucky enough to have avoided smashing my face on the shiny metal steering wheel.

At first thought, I suspected we'd hit a submerged mangrove stump, because new-fallen tree trunks were common along the water's edge.

From the bow, Robert Dean spun to me. "What in the heavens was that?" he asked with startled wide eyes.

My knuckles were clenched around the wheel. I shared his anxiety. "I have no dang clue."

"We sure hit somethin'," my friend said.

I faced the stern intensely. "No doubt." Then I used the jack plate and raised the engine, followed with the trim motor. Only up halfway, the jack plate's motor bogged down, struggling to lift the sixty-horsepower engine. The stern was being pulled under.

Robert Dean leaned closer. "Sounds like something's caught."

"Not sure what it could be. I don't remember any debris in this cut."

His eyes were alert. "You sure?"

"I'm pretty sure," I answered. "But it's been a while since I've ran back here, so who knows."

Robert Dean's eyebrows perked. "Maybe it's one of those friggin' sea cows."

"Manatee?"

"Never know…" my friend said.

"Hope not," I said, peeking down to the water, looking for plumes of red mud.

Robert Dean stepped in behind me. "Wait!" he said, pointing. "Looks like the prop might be caught on something."

I saw it. "Yeah, I'm going in."

My friend moved aside as I opened a hatch where I'd stowed my wading boots. Then I remembered that the previous day I'd removed the boots to clean after chartering the Wisconsinites. I returned astern and made for the jump when Robert Dean snatched my arm at the elbow.

"Hey, Shamus?"

"What?"

"If you die, I get the skiff, cool?"

"Funny," I said, rolling into the waist-high murk. "Now keep a lookout while I check it out." The water's temperature was close to a bath as I waded to the engine and reached under, pawing for the lower unit. "Looks like the skeg is caught on something underneath." While inspecting the lower end, I worked a hand to the propeller. Something felt out of place. "Feels like some sort of rope material."

"You need a knife?"

"Hang on a second," I said and continued to explore the lower end of the engine, tugging at the unknown material, searching for a spot of weakness—found none.

Robert Dean craned for a visual, holding my Spyderco blade in easy, reachable length. "Take this, it'll do yah, and cut right through whatever the hell that is." He eyed the knife's metal. "What's this, a fifteen-degree blade?"

"It is, and it'll cut you real easy if you're not paying attention." I took the knife, handle first, then lowered it to the rope, and using the other hand, pulled slack away from the skeg and began to cut. After removing bits of rope, I held it above the water for examination.

"Looks like some kind of twine," Robert Dean noted from over my shoulder.

I handed it up and continued slicing. "I think this stuff might be fouling the prop. It's wrapped tight. Not sure this will work without taking the prop off and clearing it that way."

"That bad, huh?" he said.

"Yeah. Do me a favor and step to the bow for a minute?"

He did and teetered the stern, elevating it enough to obtain a detailed inspection. As suspected, the material had wound deep into the propeller's shaft. Frustration won and I gripped a large handful and ripped it clear, then showed Robert Dean the dripping clump. It appeared to be some sort of netting.

My friend inspected the rope. "Oh, man…" he said, rolling the material between his fingers.

"What?" I asked anxiously.

"I know what this stuff is…"

"What is it?" I asked.

"Looks like palm fiber."

"Palm fiber?"

"Yeah, go ahead and give me another look at that necklace fish thing you got hangin' around your neck."

I reached behind my neck, removed the necklace, and flung it at him.

He snatched it out of the air. "Oh yeah, this looks like the same stuff."

I faced him. "So, what does that mean?"

"Not sure," he answered, then flung the necklace back.

My expression was flat. "Check this out…" I handed him a larger section of the netting from the propeller, "See if you can figure it out."

After a short observation, he said, "Now would you look at this—could be some kind of old-fashioned hunting technique, to catch fish."

"Hunting technique, to catch fish?" I asked, now perturbed.

"What do *you* make of all this, then?" my friend asked. "There seems to be somethin' strange goin' on right now."

"Yah think?" Aggravation was settling in.

He glanced suspiciously down the creek. Whispered, "Have you ever heard of people running nets in these waters?"

"No—not this type of net," I whispered back. "It's illegal."

He scanned the area again. "Well, looks like we might have caught some poachers, no?"

My blood began to boil. "You might be right."

"Keep an eye out, they may not be far off…"

I had my hand running along the shaft of the propeller. "I'm not sure we'll be able to get this untangled without special tools … which I don't have on the skiff."

"Let me guess, they're back on the ol' houseboat?"

"You got it."

"Shamus, that's not very captain-like."

"Funny. I keep all necessary tools when out with a *paying* customer. I removed the toolbox when I cleaned her out yesterday morning."

"From here…" He glanced down the narrow creek. "…how far would you say it is back to the houseboat?"

"It's about two miles or so."

"Think that's wade-able?" he asked.

"Sure, but it'll take a couple hours … at least."

"Well, what do you reckon our other options are?"

"How strong are you feeling?" I asked, gripping the twenty-foot white push pole mounted on the gunwale clips.

"That's goin' be a mighty long push … that's for sure."

Up at the early morning sky, alternatives flashed in my head. To wade back to the houseboat was an option, but the slowest. Flares—nope … whistle—laughable. To call Sara was an option, but as of right now, too dangerous. That left just one option, the push pole.

I grinned. "Yup, hope you don't get tired."

My friend projected a puff of air. "How far did you say it was?"

"Maybe a mile and a half."

He reached for the push pole and asked why I didn't have a trolling motor.

"Don't need one," I said from in the water.

"I beg to disagree, my ol' buddy. See that?" He pointed toward the engine. "That's FUBAR, so it appears you do *need* one—*right* now."

"How do you figure?" I asked, leading him.

"I do believe we're stranded with a fouled prop, and I sure would bet a friggin' trolling motor might come in mighty handy right now … so I'd say that you *do* need one."

"Nah."

"Yeah…"

"Nah. I've got you to pole us."

"I'll make a deal with you," he said. "We split it. I'll go ahead and take the first mile or so, then you finish it off once we get on out to the open."

"Let's just see how tired you get before we start making deals." I stood in waist-high water wiping mud from the propeller. "My sea-spine's acting up, so using the push pole isn't ideal."

My friend looked at me with serious doubt in his eye. "Are you serious, Shamus?"

I nodded rapidly. "As dick cancer. See, using the push pole and throwing a cast net for many years has taken its toll, friend, and the fish gods have come to take payment."

After our disgruntled agreement, he took the push pole, ascending the poling platform. As I ascended into the skiff, my foot snagged on something. I lowered back into the water and lifted my leg.

"Look at this," I said, pulling on a long-roped mesh.

"What?"

"Looks like this rope material stretches all the way across the creek."

From atop the poling platform, my friend saw it too. "Doesn't surprise me. Poachers will do just about anything to make a catch."

"Poachers … riiiight," I mumbled, letting the rope go, and boarding the vessel.

Robert Dean lowered the pole into the water, pressed down, and sent us forward. After a few minutes to acclimate, he soon found the proper technique and managed to skim us in a straight line.

Still fresh, the stagnant morning air was cool and crisp. Back in the narrow, breezeless creek, I perched on the tip of the skiff's bow and scanned into the water ahead for anything related to the mesh netting. Full daylight was incoming, but teetered in a state of limbo, to where I'd soon need sunglasses.

The tide began moving against Robert Dean as he pressed on. For every two feet he won from the current's pull, it claimed back a foot.

I said, "Current's moving pretty good, huh?"

"Surprised you can tell from down there," he said in strain from the poling platform.

"I just want to tell you, you're doing a hell of a job—"

My friend crouched in a flinching reaction. "What in the heck was that, Shamus … LOOK!"

"What?" I said startled, ducking as though a bomb whistled through the air.

He began hammer-pointing into the mangroves. "There … in the woods!"

I slipped astern. "Mangroves."

"Yeah, mangroves." He now whispered: "Thought I saw a little kid."

"A little kid … what?"

"Yeah, right through them limbs, about twenty foot back … balancing on a dead mangrove tree."

I grinned. "That's probably just some residual apple pie."

"Shamus, I'm serious. I saw someone." My friend focused off starboard, fixated into the green thicket. His voice lowered close to a whisper. "They was right there! By that white mangrove log, about five foot up … look like a girl. Had long hair, and she looked mighty dirty."

I peered through the bush. "I'm not sure there's even any place to stand back in these mangroves. Far as I know, it is all swamp."

Robert Dean dug the twenty-foot push pole down deep, using it as an anchor.

I disagreed. "I say we just keep on moving."

"I'm tellin' you, I seen someone!"

"Okay, I believe you, but let's just move out a little further. I know a spot up ahead that may have dry land. This low, incoming tide, we should be able to hop out and look." This was partially true, I did know of an area up ahead that, at the wicked lows of winter, might have a stretch of dry ground to stand on, but it wouldn't be accessible at this time of year. My goal was to lure Robert Dean's attention to where I needed it, which was poling back to the houseboat fast and un-fouling the propeller. Worst case scenarios, if we did encounter violent poachers, we'd be helpless and hopeless without motorized propulsion.

I said, "Just past this next point there should be some dead, dry mangrove logs we can hop onto."

My friend kept an arcane stare pinpointed toward the mangroves.

My tone suggested urgency: "Let's keep it going, shall we?"

His stare relinquished, and he removed the push pole from the muck and heaved the skiff into the incoming tide.

I said, "We'll be able to see much better from this other spot. I mean, if there *are* poachers and they have a kid—or whatever—then it'll be better to confront them with a working engine, no?"

"I suppose…"

On our way to the mangrove point one-hundred feet ahead, Robert Dean was eyeballing into every gap of green mangroves. The skiff continued to move forward, so I said nothing.

We rounded the corner and there they were—four men sitting rigid in a dug-out canoe, their backs straight as pilings, their eyes fixed ahead like carved idols set to guard the waterway.

My mouth dropped. "What the fu—"

Robert beat shifted on the polling platform. "Looks like we found 'er poachers," my friend mumbled.

"Not good," I answered.

As we drew closer on a steady, silent drift, the men were shirtless, tanned deep, had long, tangled hair, and all four men were wearing red armbands.

My friend ceased poling and dug one end of the push pole into the marl beneath the skiff.

The men appeared guarded, watchful—as did we. Their canoes slowed as they assessed our presence. They wielded long wooden spears; each tipped with a rock carved to a point like an arrowhead and bound with strips of fiber.

My friend whispered, "What do you *make* of these guys?"

These men didn't hold their ground as did we. They let their canoes drift closer, a wise usage of the current. My heart raced. The adrenaline floodgates opened, my breathing rate rose, and my eyes pulsed. The closer they came, the less sense I could make. Their faces were clean and shiny—their hulk was obvious.

The situation sharpened into clarity as we closed the gap. Their faces were etched with experience but spoke of seriousness. I glanced back at Robert Dean, whose expression seethed with confusion.

His eyes caught mine, and he whispered from the corner of his mouth, "Are you seein' what I'm seein'?"

"Yes."

At our voices, each man in the canoe raised and aimed their sharp-pointed spears directly at us.

Pulling out the dug-in push pole, my friend made the first move and let the skiff float freely. The water swept it, spinning the bow. The men took note. One of them, in the lead canoe, dipped an oar-like shaft into the water and tried to slow his vessel. The two boats behind him, loaded three men each, followed his lead.

Time seemed to inexplicably stop. All I heard was my friend drawing deep breaths—and not the soothing kind—the kind that pitched uncertainty. By way of current and tide, the three canoes were closing in.

I suggested, "Maybe you should reverse us or something?"

"Okay … then what? Is there another way out?"

"Not really, no."

He inhaled, held it, and as he exhaled frustratingly, anchored the push pole. The skiff's bow drifted with the current, slowly rotating the boat counterclockwise. Once it had turned, Robert Dean lifted the pole free. "Now what?" he asked.

"Let's be careful, *non*-threatening. And just move away, deeper into the creek."

"Then we'll be trapped."

"You got a better idea? Let's just be cool and see if they even follow us."

After a few minutes facing in the opposite direction, my friend checked behind the skiff. "They're movin' with us … I think they want to talk or somethin'…"

I didn't look. "Let's just keep going. Maybe they'll get the point that we mean no harm, turn away, and leave us alone."

Robert Dean shook his head. "I *doubt* that."

The further we went, the further *they* went. We then arrived back to the area where the propeller had been fouled. Threatening, the males drifted closer, and sensing our weakness, seemed to gain confidence. Our options were running low. Being outnumbered, I wasn't sure if cornered, we could even fight our way out. I glanced behind us one more time and reached into the console for my cell phone, to now call Sara, then the cops. A big circle with a line through told me that I had no signal. Robert Dean saw me.

"Anything?"

I remained silent, jaw clenched, shook my head NO.

"Figures," he said—then reached into a pocket, coming up empty. I remembered him leaving his cell phone behind in the houseboat on purpose. "Live free," he had said. With no way to call for help, our luck was out.

Our last point was fast approaching. I knew from fishing here many times that the creek dead-ended into a large mangrove hedge that, ironically, was the target of today's fishing. "We're the ones being caught today," I mumbled.

"Isn't this the last bend before the fishin' spot?" Robert Dean asked.

"Yup," I replied.

"Didn't you say the spot you wanted to fish was at the *end* of this creek?"

"I did yes."

"Hmmm … so correct me if I'm wrong, but now we're about to be out of creek … but at the same time … up it?"

"That would be correct," I said.

Before replying, Robert Dean checked on the marauders. "Perfect."

"Yup."

"So, that's it, we've got nowhere to go?" he said, banging the push pole onto the metal of the poling platform. "We're fricken trapped?"

"Looks like it," I said, trying to peek back at the men.

My friend's lungs filled with frustrating air. "Well … seems like I'll be havin' to activate some Smoky Mountain justice."

Before I could spit out a well-thought reply, Robert Dean poled the skiff around the final bend, and to our disbelief, ten canoes, holding four-to-five men each, sat afloat, waiting—all wearing the same red armbands and wielding identical spears.

"What shall we do now?" Robert Dean asked.

I shrugged. "How would I know? But just be cool, no sudden movements."

Robert Dean voice rose to an intense shrill. "Give me your gun, man."

"Gun? You know I don't own a gun!"

"Okay," he whispered intently, "…then give me your knife."

"Knife?" I reached for the Spyderco knife in my pocket, and while handing it over, accidentally dropped it into the water.

The canoers tightened up, compressing their spread.

"There goes that," Robert Dean said.

"I'm so pissed right now."

"What about a fillet knife … or bait knife. You got one of those?"

"Everything's in the houseboat!"

"What?"

"There might be a rusty old bait knife in the front hatch."

"Good, good," my friend mumbled in thought. "That's what we need right now. Can you hand it to me?"

"Hand it to you?" My words chirped by pure accident, and realizing my mistake, I lowered back to a whisper, "I'm not sure any more sudden movements are a good idea right now unless you want to be skewered!"

All I heard from Robert Dean was a dry, forced swallow. After what seemed like an hour, he whispered, "We're screwed."

Chapter Six

I wriggled through bush, cut under mangrove branches, and swatted off gnats and no-see-ums while a sharp stone point pressed into my back. The pressure of the spear's tip, on the verge of breaking skin, applied the right amount of jab force to keep me walking straight and doing what they commanded.

Some men walked barefoot. Others wore interesting types of footwear—snug animal hide wrapped around their tan feet. They moved through the trees like lemurs, smooth and dauntless, confident on their destination and footing. The path widened as we trekked deeper into the mangrove forest.

These men in the canoes had forced us to go with them. They spoke no language I'd ever heard and dressed like no other I'd ever seen. To communicate to us, they waved the spears—pointing them directionally while speaking in an unknown tongue.

After we trudged for what seemed like an hour, we arrived at a parking lot-sized, ten acre clearing. The ground crackled under our feet as they continued to tout and shuffle us across the shell ground like trophy tarpons.

We passed hordes of people, including small groups of women who were escorting pairs of little, happy, unclothed children. The women were topless, except for their eloquent, moss-overlaid, rawhide skirts.

As I paused to stare, the spear's tip prodded between my shoulder blades, forcing me to move on. Walking was difficult as they'd bound our feet using the same netted material as the fouling net that allowed us no more than baby steps at a time.

"Where are you people takin' us…?" Robert Dean said from a short distance behind me. "This ain't right! Hello? Hello?"

I picked up early on that these people didn't understand the same idioms as we, so up to this point the only thing my friend conveyed was hostility.

Behind, I glanced to inspect the single file of men. They were ushering Robert Dean like me, but due to his size and aggression, they had doubled up on him. He walked awkwardly, having bound ankles, and both of us had our hands tied in front of our bodies.

Deeper into the village, behind mangroves and slash pine trees, large, open-air dwellings surrounding the enclosed land. Some of them were two-story houses, where makeshift wooden ladders lead to lofts. Their roofs were palm frond-thatched, and a brownish material used for stucco resembled wet mud.

As open as the village perimeter was, they'd created plenty of shade by weaving palmetto fronds together, stringing them across multiple sable palms.

Ahead, outlines of people stood in the shade like shadows on the street—some male, others female, most of an unknown age, and all of whom appeared identical.

Our observation quickly ended as the lead man jerked my arm and ushered me into a hut. He had the strength of a Greco-Roman wrestler, so I didn't resist.

Once in the hut, they held me still until the lagging group escorting Robert Dean entered.

They positioned us side-by-side.

"I'm warning you, buddy. Hands off!" Robert Dean threatened.

I leaned to his ear, whispered, "I'm not sure these guys know what the hell we're even saying!"

Once they had us lined up, the man with three red armbands spun us, his gaze darting between our faces. Back and forth he went—from Robert Dean to me—his expression clouded with confusion. He spoke to us in a bizarre language. His tone suggested a question.

My friend spoke. "I think he's trying to ask us someth—"

The man then slapped Robert Dean's shin using the spear he held. My friend winced in pain and dropped painfully to a knee with bound ankles. The man bent and shouted something into his face.

My friend's wince now turned into a soft laugh. "What … is … goin'… on … here?"

The leader's attention focused on me, inches from my face. He had black stripes under his eyes like a baseball player, and his wrapped, matted hair wound up to a ponytail, which stunk like stale laundry. He was shirtless but a small cloth covered his loins. With his scarred arms covered in insect bites, I wondered about repellent. His long, bony fingers couldn't have been mistaken for anything other than broken and improperly aligned afterwards. In addition, his fingernails were dirty and crusted as though he'd been digging in the dirt. The smell emitting off him was unbearable, and when he talked, his mouth opened, revealing only pieces of teeth stained the color of corn.

He blinked, mind calculating as he stared into faint eyeballs behind the mirror of green lenses. On the way in, not one person had been wearing any sort of eye protection. I raised my bound hands to my face and removed the glasses.

The surrounding men sighed at the revelation. I placed them back on.

Unimpressed, the lead man signaled a lower-ranking man to leave the hut—maybe to retrieve someone or carry a message. After the door slapped shut, he faced down at Robert Dean, who was rubbing a red-purple welt ballooning on his shin.

"What you do that for anyhow?" my friend asked.

As if Robert Dean never said a word, the presumed leader lifted my sunglasses and glowered into my eyes, then moved his eyeballs down to my gray-hooded Columbia fishing shirt. His curiosity overcame him, and he reached for it. When he did, the three other men leaned in, clutching spears, squinting, stretching for a better view. When his hand reached one inch from my arm, he looked me in the eye again, a subtle ask for permission. Through the sunglasses, I nodded using a non-hostile expression. He understood, went the remaining inch, and felt the fabric.

He recoiled as though touching something hot and shouted at the others. Then his curiosity lured him back to me, then to my black shorts. He compared his clothing, and then back at mine. He reached for my shorts, touching the unknown fabric. He made the same comment to his partners. One by one, they each patted it with a finger. Microfiber must have been new to them. The last man recognized something in my pocket, leaned back, slid into a guarded position. He jabbed his spear so close my face, I nearly tasted the stoned tip. Their leader reached for my pockets. Skeptical of what he might find, he motioned to his subordinates to reach—all of whom shared the same frightened eyes.

The vibe seemed to be souring like a dead baitfish, so I took a chance and inched up my tied hands to signal that I'd be more-than-willing to empty my own pockets. All men tightened up again and straightened their spears forward to my face.

Robert Dean was staying low on one knee. "Don't do it. I wouldn't trust these people none! I've seen their scrounging type back in my mountains!"

The men this time let him speak but seemed focused, confused about his white flashy teeth clacking with every projected word. The more pissed and upset Robert Dean became, the more his teeth wobbled loose. One man reached with his fingers into his own mouth.

My friend rose, continued, "Back home these freeloaders always be trespassing on my property ... stealing all my ginseng. They have no reas—" As soon as Robert Dean's mouth made for that last syllable, the leader, wearing the three red armbands, slapped him again, hard across the shin—he collapsed.

I extended my hand, gave my friend an "easy buddy," then rotated my palms up toward the men.

"Okay, okay." In the gentlest way I knew how, I conveyed my trustworthiness through expression and signaled to the leader that I would reach into my own pocket.

Just as I reached the edge of my pants, barging through the hut's door stirring up a cloud of dust, the man he'd sent away had returned. He wasn't out of breath, but it was obvious he'd hurried. His reports were to the man who wore the three red armbands. He said something in a tender voice—but not before a short pause to find caution and compose a proper, subordinate tone.

What he told the leader, I didn't have a clue, but he received a reaction. The leader faced Robert Dean, then toward me, a type of ocular intimidation. My eyes stayed locked. I wasn't letting him win this one. He broke first and led the men from the tent. The rickety door slapped shut and locked with a flimsy latching.

The size of the hut compared to that of my lanai, except for the low ceiling. Above, they covered the roof in pine tree needles and overlaid it using dead mangrove branches. Above our heads, strings of pine needles dripped down from the roof like stalactites. I'm six-foot-tall and my head about hit. It smelled like dirt and pine and was no doubt escapable because sporadic weavings of dead palm fronds created thin, see-through walls. It wasn't built strong enough or weatherproofed as the other dwellings that filled the camp. Dozens of small slits let in light that allowed outside visibility.

I peered through one of the slits to see a guard standing three feet from the door. He wasn't a large or muscular man; stood maybe five-foot tall, but appeared fast on his feet, wiry, agile. He wasn't set guard to stop us; he guarded to alert in the event of our escape. He appeared young, uncorrupted, and by his wandering attention, I'd say he'd reached mid-teens. He was distracted easily and played with the spear as if it were a sword—sparring with an imaginary friend. A few females passed in the distance; he noticed and straightened himself.

I said, "I think the red bands are a type of insignia or something—a ranking maybe."

"Yeah?" my friend said, lying flat on his back.

"Yes. Got to be."

"Well, that tall, inconsiderate, long-haired hippie sure as heck seems to be in control, that's for sure."

Robert Dean performed a scrupulous stumble to his feet, in obvious pain from the shin slap. He fought with tied hands, staggered, stood, and dusted off his bare arms, sending a small cloud into the air. "What in the world is goin' on here?"

"I haven't got a clue." I paused and bit a nail in thought. "Maybe we're being quarantined or something?"

"Quarantined?" he asked. "I don't know, but I've got a strange feelin' about all this."

I peeked out a slit in the hut. "You and me both."

Robert Dean stamped his feet. "I think we should make a run for it."

"Run for it?" I asked.

"Yes, this pathetic excuse for a jail, or whatever, couldn't hold a flippin' baby." Robert Dean grabbed a hold of the door's wooden crossbar and shook. The whole hut wobbled. Small pine needles fluttered to the ground.

"Stop that," I said, reaching for a beam that seemed to hold up the roof. "I don't think it's meant to *physically* hold us here. I think it's more symbolic, that if you're in here, then you're meant to stay *put* … so let's, for the immediate future, try *not* to draw attention to ourselves, okay?"

"That's what you said back on the skiff…"

"I know, but let's just think this out for a minute."

"Hey, you ain't the one gettin' beat on the shins. Let them untie us and we'll go toe to toe, man to man, mountain style. See how strong they are."

"Mountain style? What's that even mean?"

"It means what it means, Shamus. We take no shit in the mountains."

Hard to argue that logic so I tried another route. "Even if you escape from this hut, then what? Run through the swamp?"

My friend's eyes darted back and forth in thought. "That's what I'm thinkin'."

I shook my head. "Even if you make it to the skiff, the prop is fouled, and you're not going anywhere."

"Then I'll just use my backwoods survival skills and lay low for a few days and then swim on back to the houseboat."

"Lay low, in the swamp? With all the creepy crawlies?"

After a few seconds pause, I realized his idea wasn't half bad, but from what we witnessed on the trek in, hundreds of people lived here.

"They'd have us hunted down in no time," I mumbled. For some reason, I didn't fear these people. From somewhere deep inside, I didn't ascribe them as a violent faction. "I don't think these people mean too much harm…"

"Easy for you to say, your stinkin' shin doesn't have a welt the size of mango on it."

"I think they reacted out of caution. You seem to put off an *aggressive* vibe."

"*Aggressive* vibe?"

"Yeah, sort of."

"Well, I was just defendin' myself," Robert Dean said—then mumbled, "Maybe you should try it."

I rolled my eyes.

"How many times have you fished the flippin' Cutoff, and you're tellin' me you never before seen these people back here?"

"No, I haven't."

He turned to me, expressing seriousness. "Well then, why did they decide to take us hostage *now*?"

"I couldn't tell you."

"I mean, what's their deal anyways? There's women walkin' 'round topless out there, just walkin' about, swingin' their breast around and whatnot. And what's with the damn naked children everywhere?"

"I can't answer that either."

"We must think of a way out, though. I think we need to get the hell out of here and call the police or somethin'."

I decided not to leave anything to chance, pulled out my cell phone, and swiped it open.

Robert Dean saw me and asked, "You callin' the cops, right?" This was less of a question than a statement.

I eyed him. "Thinking about it."

"I'd say that's the smartest thing to do. Tell 'em we've been captured by some gang of homeless maniacs and we're about to get tortured or even murdered. That should get 'em here in a jiffy."

Answerless, I checked the status of the guard to be sure he wasn't paying attention—then dialed 911. The phone let off a long tone—NO SIGNAL. I tried again—the same result.

Robert Dean was peering out to the camp through the gaps in the walls. He rubbed his shin and asked, "Well ... they comin'?"

"No signal," I replied.

"I knew it," he said, balling his hands and swinging his fists in frustration. "Just figures there wouldn't be a fricken signal at this very moment. Just figures…"

"Yeah, this area isn't a dead zone. I usually have a cell signal here."

I strained to feel the small welt on my back that I received from Three Bands on the way in, tried to harness its realness. The welt was real—no doubt about it. Robert Dean's bruised shin was also real.

"So ... now what?" he asked.

I didn't answer but focused on the guard, then surveyed the pine-needled roof and questioned if sneaking was an option.

I said, "You said something about making a run for it?"

"Oh, now you're interested?"

"Calling for help is out of the question," I said. "So, we need other options."

"I've got an option. You distract that little shit, and I'll sneak behind him, put him in a chokehold."

Not amused, I dared to ask, "Then what?"

My friend peered out one of the slits in the thin wall. Only his eyes could be seen, well-lit from a rectangle of sunlight. He faced out, scanning. "We use him for leverage."

"Leverage?"

"Yeah, we make a deal with these hobo's, okay? We'll let their precious guard go unharmed *only* if they release *us* unharmed. We'll promise not to tell anyone 'bout this little tax evasion commune they got goin' on in exchange for a free tow back to the houseboat."

I pondered the idea for a few seconds. "I don't think these people are the negotiating type. Plus, I'm not sure they even speak English. How are they going to understand us?"

"I'm sure once they see we've captured one of their own they'll be more open-minded to learn." He released a flap of palm frond, shutting the small slit.

My friend's idea wasn't bad but for now we don't need to sink to violence—yet. I had a hunch the leader was the type who'd appreciate a negotiation first.

"We've got to find a way out," my friend said, back to the slits.

The next hour we remained silent, both intermittently checking through the slits in the wall. Robert Dean mentioned he was thinking of a way to take hold of the guard.

After a good ponder, I had nothing, no idea other than to try Robert Dean's plan. "Okay, I think you should try your chokehold."

He peeked up, astonished I'd agreed. "You serious?"

"Just make it a loose chokehold." I pointed up a finger. "No reason to hurt the kid."

He raised his chin in confidence. "My shins would disagree."

"What about the this?" I bent over and jerked the loosening palm fiber that tied our ankles. "This ain't exactly comfortable." I then peeked out at the kid set a guard, who was distracted, picking at something on his toe. "Actually, scratch the chokehold. Let's just take a chance and bolt toward the skiff. They might find us not worth the trouble."

Robert Dean stepped to the shanty door, shook it again, lighter this time. "I could smash right through this."

"No smash," I warned. "But is there a way to open it without making it too obvious?"

He let go of the door. "What's with all the secrecy, Shamus?"

I stepped in to inspect. "Easy, there's no reason to give them another reason to smash your legs if we don't make it, right?"

Robert Dean had no argument. He bent and began to loosen the palm fiber around his ankles. He pulled in strain. One after another the strands broke, and after a few seconds, he was freed. I took to mine but had no luck. Under my foot, I found an opened oyster shell. The sharp lip worked well, and I used it to free my feet, then Robert Dean sliced the fiber wrapping my wrists.

"That was easy," I mumbled.

My friend balled the fibers and tossed them into a corner, then as though a locksmith, examined the door and its ability to lock.

"See anything?"

"Not yet," he whispered. "Gotta let me work!"

By work, my friend meant forcing a fist through a wide slit in the door and feeling for a latch on the other side.

I peeked for the juvenile guard through an adjacent slit. He was swirling the spear like a baton. "Feel anything?"

He'd made it shoulder deep, arm bent, pawing at the lock. "You can't rush genius…"

"If you're going to make a move, now's the time. Our guard out there is very distracted."

Robert Dean's mouth strained, lips pulled tight, composite teeth shown to the gums. There was some noise where his arm flailed on the opposite side of the door—hollow wood on wood. The door shook. We could have easily smashed through it.

"Got it!" Robert Dean stood and tested the door.

"It's unlocked?"

"Sure is." He opened it halfway and quickly shut it. Multiple limbs fell on the outside of the door.

"You broke it?"

"Shamus, it's fine. These mud lovers'll never notice."

I eyed the guard. He was farther from the door, having dropped the baton, where it tumbled away.

"You first," I hurried.

Robert Dean realized he was indeed to be the first and peeked out the slit for himself.

I encouraged. "The only thing between us and freedom is that kid." I nodded outward.

His silence indicated hesitancy.

I smiled. "It's unlocked now, let's go."

"We are *goin'*! Hang on, would yah?" He began to massage his shin. "Making sure the legs are a go, is all."

"I'll be right behind you."

Robert Dean inched to the handle and pushed the door open. I stood closely behind and when I detected his reluctance, I bumped him. He sprinted. I tried to follow but tripped, rolled over the limbs Robert Dean had ripped off the door. My friend had made good distance and disappeared behind a distant hut, then I heard him cussing. Robert Dean appeared again, running across the trail, followed by two men; only to disappear behind another hut on the opposite side. More cussing and he appeared, now followed by four men. His only path was to head back to me.

"Shamus, run!"

I did no such thing and splayed out on the crunchy ground. As Robert Dean approached the hut full bore, the petite guard swung the baton, hitting my friend in the chest, clotheslining him to the shell-laden floor. His head flopped two feet from mine.

"Told you we shouldn't have run," I said.

We were then dragged back into the hut and bound again with the same palm fibers.

A few long minutes passed then the door flap swung open, and Three Bands barged in and with hate in his eyes, pointing his spear at us. Robert Dean jumped to my side, massaging his ribs. Behind Three Bands, entered the four tall and skinny men. They held positions as though waiting for instructions.

Three Bands raised the spear and swung the tip in our direction. He stared, angered by our attempt to escape. He said something, but the instructions weren't for Robert Dean or me, they were for the four men inching closer to us. And now noticing our size, reluctantly, each took an arm.

Robert Dean became tense.

I attracted his attention. "Easy ... just relax," I whispered.

My friend stood on edge—the men sensed it. "We're in some shit now…"

Taken by each arm, they forced us out of the hut and into the high sun where the heat was as though surrounded by lava.

They forced us through the village at high speed, and at times, dragging us on our feet. An uncomfortable parchedness developed as we went on through the permeable sun.

These men kept an incredible pace—they walked tall, fast, and strong. They brought us past countless huts that surrounded the perimeter. Three Bands had his pointed stone so tight it was about to skewer me like a Shamus kabob.

Robert Dean remained quiet. For all we knew, we could be poised for release, but as we passed the small path that they used to bring us in, those expectations faded, and the anxiety of the unknown returned.

We shuffled along and again they whisked along the perimeter of the camp, showed off, paraded like a prize—this time clockwise. The perimeter seemed never-ending. Toward the center of the camp sat an enormous building, towering above all the smaller, fringe dwellings. The ground floor was entirely wide-open. Massive wooden columns rose like ancient sentinels, bearing the weight of everything below. Three Bands must have sensed my curiosity and tossed me a callous elbow. I faced forward and kept marching as his ever vigilant prodding was a constant reminder to stay on task.

We were dragged, forced past a row of similar dwellings that were open on the ground floor, with upper levels enclosed and raised on columns. The structures appeared to be cypress tree-construction, which they may have imported, along with hundreds of gumbo limbo trees that they had used as trusses.

From the unrelenting heat, I heard Robert Dean ask, "Can we please get some water? Aqua?" He spoke as if talking to the man behind him. They didn't respond, so he began physical drinking motions to communicate his parchedness, raising his tied hands to his mouth and tilting. He received a not-so-surprising answer. One of Three Bands' subordinates jabbed the spear into the small of his back.

"You guys are goin' be sorry, I'm tellin' yah. Don't think you know who you're messin' with."

I again drew Robert Dean's eyes to mine and mouthed, "Give it up."

At the northern edge of camp, we came upon a clearing lined with long, weathered picnic tables arranged in tidy rows. A handful of women sat at them filleting fish. They looked up, to grasp a fleeting view of what the hunters had brought home. I mumbled, "Hope were not the main course…" Pounds of snook and redfish spread wide, having been recently sliced, seeped pools of blood into the wood of the tables, bleeding along the edges. I glanced at Robert Dean's wide eyes. He saw me. The makings of a feast was obvious.

I said under my breath, "No way those are legal."

More surprising than the illegal poaching of snook and redfish was the impressive manmade canal leading up to the fillet stations. Canoes lined the canal, all of which were empty and primitive in their design—dugouts—fresh from the land. They built a perfect layout. Fisherman just had to row up to the bank, offload the day's catch, and lay them onto the awaiting fillet stations where the women were ready, sharpening knives made from honed-sharp mollusk shells.

The canal wasn't wide, maybe fifty feet. On each side they'd sliced, diced, and spread apart the tangled mangroves leading up to the beach. The green rim at their slice points was vivid, a stark indicator of their recent severance from the larger limbs.

After noticing their advantageous destruction of protected mangroves trees, and the excavation of numerous salt-resilient roots that were a protected barrier from the sea, it became clear that they'd carved an actual canal system through the mangroves. The tide rose here high enough to reach the embankment, so dredging a reasonably wide mangrove path fashioned its own canal. These homesteading villagers had been diligent.

They kept us moving but my legs, tied at the ankles, could only spread inches apart. The material they'd used to tie my hands began to slice into my wrists.

I glanced up at the sun, setting my sight to a blinding darkness. These recent events were happening at a rapid speed, and I'd failed to evaluate our current predicament properly. My mental brain hadn't processed the events as quickly as my physical body. But one thing I was sure of was: Robert Dean and myself had been taken by some sort of secret society—the kind of society that doesn't pillage but displays an intelligent usage of Mother Earth's gifts.

They appeared to have harnessed the basic needs for survival—food and water. Shelter was there—but primitive— one could survive without it. But food and water? The most hardened survivalist would struggle to live in this heat for more than a week or two without it. Those they'd figured out well within the community.

Twenty yards beyond the fish offloading station sat five dug fire pits. Again, using long wooden poles, only women attended the fires. They stabbed, prodded, and stoked the coals again and again; embers floated off like flickering fireflies. The woman stared, but not by surprise. Out of empathy they stared at us, out of sadness—expressions somber and restrained. I fixed on one woman, face streaked with dirt and soot, a skirt of tangled moss hanging in uneven strands around her hips. Her hair, long and black, and if touched might feel like yarn. Clear beads of sweat gathered at her temple, catching the light before they slipped down her dark skin. Her small breasts sagged like deflated balloons, large black nipples pointing to the ground. Her motions were stiff and robotic, and as we closed in, I mumbled, "I hope she's not stoking the fire for us."

Chapter Seven

Not all the kidney-shaped fire pits had live fires. Some had been extinguished, while the ashes of charred remains were scooped and dumped into a hole dug beside the pit.

Three Bands dictated my direction with the spear using uneased prodding at the small of my back. If I started to sway out of line, the stone tip scraped across my skin and pressed on either side of my spine to steer me in his desired direction. Although I hadn't yet felt blood, it wasn't far from flowing.

We passed the canal, the fish unloading area, and the fire pits. A warm breeze streamed across my face, so I breathed in the wind and exhaled to snag a small bit of moisture. The air in my lungs felt heavy and wet. My head began throbbing—dehydration was likely settling in and my ancles felt like I had ten pounds of sinkers tied to them.

Behind me, Robert Dean was also suffering the effects of waterlessness. It had been several long hours since our capture, and on any normal fishing trip, I'd have already gone through multiple bottles of water. A bead of sweat traced down my forehead and fell across my cheek. I still had the ability to sweat—a good sign, for now. I knew our pace had to be slowed. Desperate to conserve a minuscule amount of energy, I tried not to focus on becoming dehydrated. Instead, I concentrated on slipping my hands into a better position, rotating my wrists, and removed the wrapped-taut fiber from the slits it had carved.

Three Bands noticed my movements and pressed on the spear.

As I walked on, my flip flops scooped up a mixture of sugar sand and shells, placing extra stress on my legs. The circumference of this strange settlement seemed to never end. Many tall people moved swiftly through well-worn paths; most walked in diligence, though completing some sort of task—a job perhaps. Young kids, no older than five or six, ran through the camp, chasing each other and playing games. They all spoke the same perplexing tongue.

After the interesting canal system, the perimeter of the camp was protected by a seven- foot, semi-tall makeshift barrier. They had used large, empty mollusk shells as building blocks, each laid identically as a bricklayer might set his bricks. The shell openings all faced outward, locked in place with a cement-like substance resembling dried mud. From a few hundred yards away, the wall stretched long and low, forming a substantial portion of the camp's boundary. It wouldn't protect much from the elements—rain, wind, or fire, but might discourage the occasional swamp creature from wondering in. Maybe its purpose wasn't for protection but show. With its graceful design, an artist, or perhaps a sculptor, had fixed the shells in place with deliberate elegance. Most were evenly aligned, though some were staggered, adding a sense of depth. The mud-ish cement-like adhesive bonded the shells together, smearing into the cracks. Although it didn't seem to be in use as any sort of defensive tool, it represented a partition of sorts—something a chain-link fence would do.

We walked side by side along the narrow path that followed the wall stretching across most of the northern border. Every twenty yards or so, thin, worn sections had eroded into shallow, step-like grooves—footholds where people could climb over or cross. The wall was tall enough to block my view, but the presence of mangroves on the far side was unmistakable.

We eventually reached a fork. One way continued ahead; the other led through a hollowed-out opening between palmettos bushes, back into the heart of the settlement. The spear scraped across my back, signaling me to move right.

I had expected the short path to lead us to the northern tip of the settlement—and it did. Looking back, we'd entered from the south and walked nearly half the camp's circumference, arriving at the northern rim. By my best estimation, it spanned two to three miles.

They escorted us through a green, leafy doorway, and after a few minutes, we arrived at the rear of a small shanty no larger than a backyard shed. Spanish moss and palm fronds wrapped the roof and curled like knotted hair. Wood from the cypress and gumbo limbo tree were tied together to frame it into a square. It might keep out the rain but wouldn't stand a chance against a hurricane.

We rounded the corner to the front of the house, where a woman swept the threshold using a homemade broom constructed from the fronds of a sabal palm. She glanced up at me and smiled, exposing rows of black, grimy teeth. Her eyes swiveled to Three Bands, who walked behind me. She lowered her head—a gesture of obeisance. As she swept, she shuffled back into the shadows of the hut.

Once the house was behind us, we joined a broader stretch of the interior perimeter trail—wide enough that, if paved, it might have passed for a road. The overhanging trees offered a pleasant shade as we walked. The path was also flat, and thick sugar sand and smashed-flat shells covered most of the walkable area. Everywhere were shells; sneaking up on someone was out of the question. The shells were large and from oysters and scallops—obviously a source of food.

We followed the shell path and continued our trek along the fringe. Three Bands and his clan of disciplined men moved across it with remarkable ease. Though Three Bands wore some kind of hide for foot protection, the others went barefoot. Their feet pressing atop the shells didn't seem to be painful—only painful for me to hear. Even though I wore sandals, shell bits gathered between my toes, slicing in the webbing of my feet.

After a few dozen yards down the shell path, we came to an area cleared of all trees—but surrounded by planted sabal palms, sagging many dead fronds. There were two entrances, one in and one out, both resembling a palmetto-constructed wedding altar. Multiple raised piles of dirt were heaps in the center—identical mounds, each seven feet long, three feet wide, and one foot high.

Robert Dean caught up, surveyed the area, then leaned closely. His breath brushed my ear as he whispered slow and deliberate, "Graves."

Beside each grave lay small, seemingly deliberate offerings—a neat stack of objects, among them a handmade rug brushed with faded red symbols. At this point, it was difficult to discern any clear motive behind all the parading. Were they marching us in circles to intimidate us for the escape attempt? First, we were captured. Then paraded through what resembled a prehistoric camp, locked in a hut for hours, and later forced to march for miles through the sweltering compound. From there, we were led to a primordial fishing dock, jostled along a shell-lined wall, and just when we thought the ordeal might be ending, brought instead to what appeared to be a cemetery. And to top it all, if they didn't give us liquids soon, neither I nor Robert Dean would have any fight left.

We'd reached what I assumed was the cemetery's halfway mark. That's when they forced us to stop and observe the burial mounds. Three Bands removed the spear from the small of my back. His mangled finger pointed to the grave, and while still facing me, I stared back, but my confusion I couldn't hide.

He stomped up to me, spoke into my face—anger filled his eyes. I could do nothing but lower my chin. The words meant nothing because I couldn't understand them, but his tone was telling another story. He pointed again toward the grave and brought his spear up, spreading it across the whole cemetery, redistributing our focus to see all the graves. I tried to send his eyes the most earnest, sympathetic, non-mocking expression I could display. It wasn't hard to understand that this was a place of death. The villagers must have come here, as anyone would, to mourn their dead.

Overwhelming heat pressed down like a thousand-pound weight. Robert Dean sagged, his face slack, eyes glazed with exhaustion. The color had drained from him, and I doubted he grasped even the foggiest meaning of what unfolded before us.

While Three Bands stood ahead, a short man walked wordlessly through the entrance carrying a dark-feathered homemade hat. He stopped and stared—lost in thought. Three Bands bowed in respect, found the sweet spot in my back, led us through the palmetto altar, granting the man respectable privacy.

*****

Once we broke beyond the arc of green palm leaves, we entered a separate path, perhaps an inner artery of the main perimeter trail.

Three Bands pushed ahead, using me like a lantern on a pole. Each jab drove me forward as if my ankles weren't bound at all, as if I could walk with a full stride. I mumbled, "Lighten up, dude."

While I grudgingly trudged along, shells under my feet crunched, crackled, and squeaked. We again passed multiple empty dwellings.

Ahead, a clan of young villagers began to walk with us like kids led out for recess. Determining their ages was difficult, and both sexes were being portrayed as males with long, straight black hair like a horse's mane. They all seem to be flowing toward the center of the colony.

Three Bands slowed us as we approached the center of the village. The large structure, which I saw during our entry, came into view through a thicket of palms. I now understood the crowd's destination. Everyone was gathering in the lower level of the enormous dwelling.

Our guides halted us fifty yards from what I assumed to be the main entrance, and forced out backs against a long-dead sable palm. They placed Robert Dean to my left, positioning two hardy men on either side of him, holding spears ready to stab. Three Bands guarded us with a watchful eye.

I was no expert, but I'd say we were about to be sacrificed in front of the whole village. Robert Dean became aware of the same thing after we locked eyes.

"Remember?" he said with tacky lips. "You agreed to my escape plan…"

"It might have worked if you didn't get caught."

"Really, Shamus?"

"Yes, really!"

Robert Dean blew off my words, raised his chin, and turned to the group. "What is goin' on here?" he said to the men. "I demand to know some answers! Wait 'till I get my lawyer on this. I'll own this place!"

I shrugged, shook my head, and mumbled, "I'd say we should keep out mouths shut."

After getting ignored, he turned to the smaller guard. "Hey, listen, bud. I'll protect you. Just let us go … cool?"

Again, I tried to silence him. "Relax, man."

"I will not relax!" he exclaimed. "I'm pretty sure these people are about to make some sort of example out of us … right here in front of the whole fricken village!

I hid my frustration. "We don't know that for sure."

"Sure. we do. I'm from the mountains, and up there we trust our gut!"

I clenched my teeth. "Well, maybe that's your problem!"

Robert Dean waved off my words and turned to the smaller guard. "Well, what's it goin' be, son?" he asked the kid—a boyish-faced kid, free of facial hair, but tall and lean—maybe sixteen.

"I don't think he can understand you, remember?"

"I couldn't give one flying muck what he understands, get it? I'm an *Amer-ri-can* and this is the *U-nited* States of *America*, and kidnapping is *il-le-gal*"

Couldn't argue that, so I maneuvered my body, shifting enough to squeeze out a glimpse of the towering structure. Three Bands stared—very observant he was, no doubt a soldier, warrior.

Nearly a minute later, a faint, distant song streamed from the mansion's direction. The voices were soft, maybe female, and seemed to catch Three Band's attention. He motioned to the man on Robert Dean's left to get us moving.

My friend resisted. "Get your hands off me! Oh? So, I'm the first one to go? This ain't right!"

My friend struggled to seize the man's hands, but they were faster and easily dodged his attempt, then one of them struck my friend's good shin with a sharp, punishing slap.

He dropped.

"I swear," he scowled from the ground. "I'm goin' get you, man." Three Bands then signaled to yoke Robert Dean up to his feet while he grimaced in pain.

I patiently waited for Three Bands' instructions, but he continued focusing on my friend, paying close attention to his ability to walk after sustaining the injury. He gave the same signal to the hulking man to my right. I went obediently.

The soldiers led Robert Dean ahead as they escorted us toward the huge dwelling. Three Bands stayed out to the far left of us, waiting to flank if we tried running, but with our bound ankles, we wouldn't get far.

Although the pain was familiar, the familiar prick of stone found its home along my back, but Three Bands wasn't the one holding the spear. The juvenile pressed using much less force. Maybe my strange appearance intimidated him. Physically, Robert Dean and I were fully grown men, and he was a child.

As we drew closer to the doorway, it became apparent that the villagers had gathered for us. The soldiers marched us down a shell path, over patches of whiter, cleaner shells, where both men and women villagers lined each side of the isle. As the song went on, our entrance was like that of a boxer making his way to the ring.

Their songs swelled as we neared the mansion's entrance. When we were no more than ten feet from the doorway, the source revealed itself. The melody had the cadence of a chant—summoning something, perhaps a god or spirit. The voices, soft and solemn, belonged to young children arranged in two even lines—ten on each side—forming a quiet passageway into the unknown. Robert Dean stopped inches before the green, leafy arc. He looked up at it.

Three Bands allowed it. Returning from the flank, he pointed the spear across the crowd, preaching something loud and authoritarian. The path then collapsed and formed a single wall, leaving us a small circle of space.

Robert Dean turned toward me, his upper body twisting to reveal a pale, expressionless face. He said nothing. In the mirrored lenses of his glasses, my own frightened face stared back.

The song grew louder, and the beat of the chants intensified. Then Three Bands swiped back the itchy moss curtain, and using the spear's stone point, pushed Robert Dean through the arc of leaf.

I was next, and before they forced me to enter, I stole a fleeting glance at the clear blue sky, and seeing no eclipse, wondered if I'd ever see one again.

Chapter Eight

I **swiped** the moss from my face using my tied-up hands while whisked through the doorway. On the opposite side of the stadium-sized mansion, lined up in long, methodical rows, numbering in the thousands, all ages of villagers were sitting quiet and cross-legged. And as Robert Dean's path led to center stage, their ominous eyes seemed to understand our possible fate.

We arrived stumbling, parched, and exhausted to where a man was sitting in a chair waiting.

My friend stood first before the man first, a delirium smile on his face. "Here we go," he mumbled.

The man's hands rested on a chair, made from what I observed to be bones. A leg bone's visible, round white condyle glistened between his fingers—he was their chief. As shocking as the bone chair was, the chief had another distinctive feature. A panther's head rested atop his own like a ceremonial headdress. Its lower jaw was missing, perhaps removed to help it sit more securely, and the eyes had been replaced with polished black stones.

The man eyed us with an authoritative glare. He raised his narrow arms, silencing the crowd while the rings of his golden bracelets rattled. His hands held steady, placating while he gazed at the obedient crowd. The crowd, from their cross-legged seat, seemed to crave for his words, awaiting instructions from their leader. The chief's head rotated outward, focusing on the most distant members, settling them with his lowering hands.

Robert Dean stance shifted.

Three Bands noticed, reacted by poking Robert Dean in the back using the spear. My friend flinched in pain. Three Bands again prodded my friend. "Ouch, crap. I'm so gonna get you."

Slowly, their chief's hands returned, resting back onto the arms of the bone chair.

A woman sitting next to the chief moved her head, rattling the shell earrings that were dangling from her ears, decorated with extravagant little spirals and circles. Her long hair was tied beneath a headband, above which a fan of feathers sprouted— arranged like a peacock's display. She wore the same style Spanish moss skirt as the others, but hers, had been colored with flowers. Shiny rings of gold circled her toes, and she sat, hands folded and seemed almost bored.

Their chief continued to sit, observing two men, who were alien in nature. A red inky dye filled in his eye sockets when his brown eyes squinted.

Robert Dean was poked once again, and this time he mumbled, "You keep doing that, I'm goin' get you, I swear," and tried half-turning toward Three Bands.

When Three Bands raised his spear to hit a homerun off my friend's shins, their chief spoke.

I couldn't, for the life of me, understand a single word. They sounded more like short, grunting syllables.

In confusion, Robert Dean looked my way—his glasses had dropped around his neck, and his eyes were wider than the Pope's on Sunday. All I could do was shrug.

My friend faced their chief. "Okay, okay … real funny. I get it. Joke's on us. Ha ha. Very funny—you win." He raised his tied wrists. "Joke's over … c'mon."

What their chief had said to Three Bands, I couldn't figure, but hearing just one word from him, Three Band's fingers whitened, cinching around the wooden spear. He slapped the back of Robert Dean's calve. Robert Dean grimaced in pain, dropped to his knees, and fell off to the side.

I closed my eyes, searching for answers. What was the meaning of this? How on earth did we get captured—in modern society—by a gang of inconspicuous off-the-grid-ers?

My eyes then spiked open when the spear found my back. It was now *my* turn before the boss. His face remained stoned as he sat, awaiting something.

"What could they possibly want?" I mumbled.

Robert Dean rolled onto his back, whispered, "Try apologizing, Shamus."

"For what?"

"The escape attempt."

"It was your idea!"

He blinked, facing up at the thatched roof. "I'm banged up good, C'mon."

I moved my hands toward my pockets.

The crowd responded in deep, loud breaths.

Three Bands poked the spear deeper, but I kept my hands moving toward my pockets.

Their chief raised his hand again, signaling Three Bands to let me continue. I picked up on it, fingered down my pocket, and removed my cell phone. The crowd reacted again with low-register whispers. My cell phone got the chief's attention, and he held out his hand.

Three Bands prodded the stone into my back.

I stepped forward, and whispers from the crowd intensified. I handed their chief the phone. He observed as though he'd never seen such a device before in his life. The woman to his right didn't seem to be the least bit interested and picked at her nails.

First thing the chief noticed was the device's weight and held it as if weighing oranges. Then, he inadvertently pressed a button, illuminating the screen. He flinched as though it had bitten him, dropped it, rose out of anger, and using the heel of his bare foot, stomped on the phone like a cockroach.

Robert Dean shook his head. "Good one, genius."

The vibe nosedived like the sinking Titanic. All my hopes of getting freed and not killed, died quicker than a pier caught catfish. It seemed I'd embarrassed the leader of the community, so I was now to pay a price.

After the phone was reduced to a pile of broken glass and plastic, the chief propped up, twisted, reached for a three-foot wooden spear that was leaning against the side of his raised chair, and vigorously pointed it out toward the direction we had been brought in. He spoke again to his crowd in a totalitarian tone.

"This can't be good," I heard Robert Dean utter as one of the men lifted him to his feet.

Three Bands instructed a lower-ranked men to usher us outside. We marched, Robert Dean in the lead, guided by three men, and me behind him. Three Bands was on my six.

They prodded us back into the sun, to a shaded area adjacent to the mansion—the crowd chanted while they followed.

W We were shoved forward to stand nervously before an enormous rock, six feet long and three feet wide that was the same size as the graves, resting three feet up, pillared by mangroves stumps. The rock was clean except for one end of it, stained in brown liquid—blood.

Bushels of large, bright green, long-stem wildflowers surrounded the sacrificial rock where their vibrant colorful petals were in total contrast to the area's somber vibe. Next to the rock stood a tall, stumped trunk of a long-dead cabbage palm, and in one section, the rind had been stripped, peeled, and small brown liquid blotches peppered the surface of the carved-out space. They were round fingertip-sized impressions, and the same color as on the rocks.

Robert Dean saw the same thing as I and began to panic. "Oh, heck no, I ain't goin' out like this!" He turned to me. "Shamus, think of somethin' quick!"

Two of the most cumbersome men in Three Bands' group took Robert Dean on each arm. He struggled, then relented as though his mind decided this had to be a sick joke. He acted as though this whole ordeal couldn't be happening, and seemed to be playing alone, like on a TV show. "Okay, you got us, ha ha … where are the cameras?" He attempted to look under the rock, but their chief's arrival stalled him.

The crowd spread apart like the Red Sea for their chief to glide up to us while his wife trailed. He pointed toward the rock and said something that sounded like a prayer.

Two men then shoved Robert Dean up to the palm tree stump. Three Bands snatched his wrist, forcing up the palm of his hand, and without hesitation, and before Robert Dean could react, pricked his index finger's tip as though taking a sample of blood. Three Bands' grip tightened and wrenched Robert Dean's wrist.

"Ouch!"

At the tip, a small drop of red blood formed. Three Bands muscled my friend's finger up to the cabbage palm stump and pressed the bloody tip against the tree and released—leaving an identical blotch.

They manhandled my friend onto the stone, his knees buckling, and laid him flat as a floating dock piling.

"It's cold, Shamus—the stone is cold." My friend was now fading into delirium. He faced me in a way a paralyzed person would while trapped in a helpless body, unable to speak coherently or communicate—desperate for help.

Without warning, a broad-shouldered, unknown man stepped forward from the crowd as the others swayed back, parting in methodical retreat. He wore a painted black, wooden mask that had a prominent and sharp, hooked nose, coming to a point as an eagle's beak. He also wore the same red armband as the others, but his was torn and faded. He clenched a lit bundle of sage in his hand. Its smoke lifted into the air as he chanted, "Oon-baba-cha, oon-dada-cha," while waving the minty sage as though to kill evil spirits. Cinched around his waist was a makeshift belt, from which hung an array of tools seemingly carved from aged bone, and strapped in place, much like a cop's pepper spray or handcuffs. The man stepped brutishly toward the stone where Robert Dean lay.

Fearing what no doubt was to come next, I spoke the first thing that came to mind. "I have food!"

Even though they didn't understand what I spoke, the urgency of my tone captured their attentions. "Wait!" I said firmly as I slipped to Robert Dean's side and held my tied hands in the air, signaling I meant no harm. "I have meat— fish!"

Ignoring my pleas, masked man paused, and using a free hand, removed from his belt the largest of all the weapons—a sharp, bone-carved cleaver.

I repeated louder, "I have FOOD!" and pointed to my mouth, then stomach, then pointed to their chief.

Masked man pivoted forward, raised the cleaver high above his head for maximum cut, and as he went for the strike, the chief grunted, held out his hand, palm up, and signaled the man to stop—he did, suspending the sharp-edged, decapitating weapon above his head.

Robert Dean opened one eye. "Am I dead?"

A suspenseful hush fell over the gathering after the crowd drew a collective breath. Black Mask, the others, and I leaned forward, waiting for the chief's magical words.

I peeked at the front row of curious onlookers with cagy eye contact. The crowd's diversity ran all the way to the back, from men, to women, to children, to women holding children, who held handfuls of breast, and also to younger males who were watching and learning from their chief and Black Mask. They all turned toward me with mounting anticipation, eager to hear of my words now that I had iced their enthusiastic, ready to inflict death, black-masked killer.

I stumbled forward again, picked a shell off the ground, and pretended to eat it. The eerily silence continued momentarily. Then from deep within the rows, one lone giggle began. And after it spread, the entire crowd began to giggle. Hearing this, I grew confident and continued my desperate charade, and using the oyster shell, slowly traced it from my mouth to my stomach—then pointed it to them, signaling I had food, and could feed them. The chief, the killer Black Mask, and Three Bands formed a closed circle and seemed to begin a discussion.

I rushed to Robert Dean's rock, mumbled, and elbowed toward Black Mask, "This guy is really primed to kill, huh?"

After a minute of talking, the group separated, and the leader, Chief, cleared his throat.

I felt compelled to continue even more desperately, and with a parched, dry mouth, I demonstrated the same eating motion repeatedly. Seconds in, one giggle began again, this time from a child in the front row, then another giggle, then a laugh, and moments later, I had given the performance of my life as the villagers laughed and cheered.

Three Bands stood statuesque as Chief gradually stepped to within two feet of my face. At maybe five feet tall, he was short compared to all the other dwellers. His cheeks were heavy, dropped down above a weathered, hairless face. He held firm ahead of me as his infiltrating stare seemed to pierce into my brain, into my thoughts. My eyes focused on his. Once they met, I realized his vibe was sociable, and mildly genial. I could see clearer now, his big cat headwear, was as I suspected, an elusive Florida panther.

I breathed slower, began to relax, then motioned to Robert Dean, "I've got this," with a lame thumbs up.

My friend seemed to feel safe and sat up, legs sliding outward, planting his tied ankles to the sandy ground. Everyone watched as he limped to my side. "Atta boy," he said, brushing off his arms. "Now what?"

I answered from the corner of my mouth. "I have no friggin' clue."

Chief slipped aside, said something to Three Bands. He gave us a nod, then drifted toward the numinous crowd, vanishing as though the mass had simply absorbed him. His wife stayed.

Three Bands raised his spear high and discussed something among his men.

Robert Dean's eyes became red, hateful. "I'm runnin' for it … I swear."

"Again?"

"Hell, yes!"

"I won't stop you."

Chief's wife slipped closer to us, wearing a long, black-feathered headband, where its lengthy thick feathers faded to white stripes. The feather's latter half thinned, coming to a point. *Primary flight feathers of a bald eagle*, I thought.

Like Chief, she was short at five foot tall. She plucked a feather from the head covering and held the pointed tip between the ends of her fingers. She feathered from my forehead to my chin, paused, then continued down to my waistline.

Robert Dean let out a slight chuckle.

I tried to remain motionless, and for reasons I couldn't explain, closed my eyes—maybe it had something to do with feeling the soft touch of tickling air. She chanted in the same rhythm as Black Mask, but with a different meaning. In a higher pitch, she pulled the chants along, leading the song.

Robert Dean chuckled again, and that drew her attention.

A crowd still surrounded us, circling under a perceptive watch. To them, we were just street performers, an act of entertainment. And the wife, the director, and Robert Dean and I—the unwilling participants.

She continued the same chant to my friend.

Three Bands waited patiently for the blessing to end.

Finally, she floated backward as though on ice and the crowd accepted her like the sea swallowing a sinking fish. In an instant the people were gone, dissipated—back to doing whatever they had been doing.

In the same instant, before I had time to make a thought, the spear found my back as the men whisked us back toward our arrival point. I staggered with my ankles tied, had tremendous cottonmouth, and felt like I'd eaten a spoon full of cinnamon. Even trying to swallow began to be a chore.

After ten minutes, Robert Dean lagged fifty feet behind, dragging his feet. The two men assigned to his escort could barely hold him up. If we didn't receive water soon, I wasn't sure how much longer he or I could hold on. These people had to have access to fresh water, a necessary product if they've survived for this long.

From out my left eye peripheral, I saw my friend, without warning, whisked down a separate path to mine, back toward the jailer hut. I stopped and pointed toward the trail.

"My friend? Where is he being taken?"

I used the same hand motion that Robert Dean tried to communicate earlier, signifying a drink request. "Drink?" He understood, and his head shook in sympathy, a signal for YES.

This was a huge breakthrough. Now we were beginning to communicate.

Without Robert Dean, they prodded me to march on.

Minutes later, just him and I reached the water's edge, near where earlier they'd taken us hostage. Three Bands froze and held out a hand, trying to communicate something. He pointed insistently toward the water, repeating the gesture again and again, but the meaning escaped me. His tone shifted, rising with a frustrating edge, and as his temper mounted, he raised the spear high into the air, then spiked it tip down into the soft sand under my feet. But before I could react, he pulled from his belt a knife carved from stone and stomped violently toward me. "Here we go," I mumbled, closing my eyes while preparing to die, but I peeked, flinched, and brought my hand up.

Three bands knelt and sliced the ties around my ankles, stripping the palm fiber cuffs from my legs.

Feeling dumb, he led me around a short mangrove bushel through knee-high water to an awaiting canoe, its bow up on the short beach, stern floating out in inch-deep water—feet away from my skiff. He pointed to the canoe and then to his mouth. He wanted me in the canoe—to produce the food I'd promised. I understood, boarded the canoe, and sat on a flimsy stringer as Three Bands took the bow, and shoved us off.

Chapter Nine

We exited the mouth of the creek into the open Myakka Cutoff. Blood filled my arms. From the bank, I'd strenuously paddled the whole way while Three Bands sat at the bow, facing me—wide eyes, wrinkled forehead, irritation had him avoiding eye contact.

Once we broke free from the protection of the mangroves, a strong breeze refreshed, wafting across my face. Regardless of the intense muscle burn, I continued paddling us out toward the middle of the Cutoff. But each sweeping gust that hit our canoe battered us back many feet.

At the bow, Three Bands gave no impression of assisting, watching me struggle as if he were an Olympic training coach. I caved out of frustration, laid the carved-wooden paddle across my lap, remained motionless, eyes pinned on his. I began finally to air-paddle, pointing to a paddle laying right next to his feet. No doubt he understood my point, but he just sat, arms crossed—his skimpy loincloth hardly covering anything.

I became irritated and decided not to paddle unassisted. Minutes later, after the wind had whisked us a hundred arbitrary yards, he finally abandoned his stubbornness and irritatingly took up the paddle. Only then did I join.

Minutes later, we found rhythm, and I aimed us toward the houseboat, which in the next fifty yards, should pop into view. The thought of its discovery suddenly covered me in fear. If it had been found—and worst case, raided—our chance of repairing the skiff and escaping would come to a disappointing end.

When we rounded the mangrove point, Three Bands spotted the houseboat first and reached straight for his spear, pointing in toward me a defensive position. "Unaababa … unaababa," he said with fierce, tight lips.

I tossed my hands in the air, "Woah, woah, "…then lowered them like telling a kid to calm himself down. My tone was soft, though soothing an angry dog. "Calm now … easy … nobody wants to hurt you."

He lowered the spear, turning tensely toward the houseboat as though confronting some great beast, then swung back to face me, eyes narrowed. Once we became within a stone's throw from the boat, I let the canoe drift. I wanted to see the houseboat first—get in, ascertain if it had been ransacked. I realized from Three Bands' mannerisms, I had to assume no one had discovered it.

I inched the canoe forward, bumping the stern pontoon of houseboat. Three Bands remains still, gripping the spear. I nodded to the taffrail, a signal to hold us against the pontoon. But as we kept drifting away, I rose, demonstrated that we needed to be secured. After we bumped ten more times, Three Bands lifted, clenched the rear metal taffrail of the big vessel, and detained the canoe tight against the houseboat.

I wasted no time bringing the stern of the canoe close to the railing and hopped off, rushed into the cabin, reached for the cooler, snatched for a bottled water, and guzzled it almost empty.

I heard footsteps behind me. Three Bands had entered in caution, head inches from touching the ceiling. He started goggling around as though stepping into a spaceship. He saw me swallowing the last bit of water while it slid down the bottle and into my mouth. My eyes were on his—watching in defensive. Now that he was in *my* domain, I could easily disable him and therefore rescue Robert Dean.

But the past had taught me otherwise…

I picked up another bottled water, and as a peace offering, held it out for him, shaking the bottle. "Water?" I asked.

His slanted eyes focused on me. Like a cat, he swiped at the bottle, dropping it to the ground, and snatched up the spear.

"Here we go again," I mumbled.

I picked up the bottle and walked to the cooler. "See?" I waved my hand through the fast-melting ice.

Three Bands leaned, noticed my hand submerged, shifting the last remaining cubes. For interest, I held up two cubes.

He focused hard on the cube forming a puddle in the palm of my hand, might as well be looking at a glowing piece of alien light. I could've used this moment of distraction as an opportunity to hurt the man, disable him, then escape to find help. He was curious at the ice as any child discovering a new toy, but his overcaution overrode ambition. Whoever these people were, they didn't get out much, and my God, the aroma fuming off this man was a nauseating mixture of mold and pungent body odor.

In an instant, I flipped the cube into my mouth and crunched down, then opened for him to see.

He smiled for the first time—an emotion other than the soldier bravado he'd been portraying, enough to let his guard down and grant me a chance to connect, to present a slice of my own world.

I squeezed the dropped water bottle and handed it to him. After a minute of wheedling, he finally held it and experienced its chill. I watched as he rolled the bottle up his cheek, an automatic response to cool the body. He knelt at the cooler, inserted a hand, scooping and splashing the melting ice. I slipped away to gather our needed repair items.

Only situation-appropriate items were necessary. First, I went to the back porch storage space and gathered the tools needed to remove the propeller from the engine and make the necessary repairs.

After all sorts of tools filled a large duffle bag, I opened a separate cooler I kept astern, icing the cobia, and before removing the massive chunks of fillet, I thought it might be easier to return to my stranded skiff by way of the houseboat's engine.

He was new to ice, so I wondered what his reaction would be once I fired up the outboard—it might cause his head to explode. It was time worth saving and I decided to risk it. I brushed past him while he fixated on the ice and moved to the helm. I pressed the key, setting off a soft click of choke, and now turned the key. To survey his reaction, I fixed my eyes on the lean, tan, wiry, ice-infatuated man.

He no doubt felt the engine's slight vibration and stopped dead with his child-like cooler splashing and crept to the spear, snatching it in a knuckle-white clench.

"It's cool, man. Just relax," I said to him.

He leaped to the stern where the engine sat idling, franticly searching for the source. He found the outboard attached to the transom and made motions to stab it.

"Don't do that." I warned, half smirking. I then left him mesmerized while I moved to the bow and pulled anchor.

Upon returning to the stern, he'd disappeared, out of sight. After not finding him in the cabin either, I returned to the stern. Only then did I notice he'd slid back into the canoe like a fiddler crab into a hole.

"It's okay, man, really," I said, smiling.

I waved to lure him back up to the houseboat, but he refused, clutching the spear, sitting at the stern of his canoe.

"Suit yourself..."

I relocated behind the helm, and now with the houseboat making way, I shifted her into gear and idled off. Once the stern line I attached to the canoe became taut, the canoe whipped straight. Three Bands clenched the sides of it as though riding down the final drop on an amusement park flume.

The sun had begun to descend, dropping west for the night, where invisible pockets of humid air lingered. A soft breeze swept across the wide-open Cutoff—a pretty sight as it wrinkled the water's surface.

My stomach rumbled in hunger. I realized that I hadn't eaten anything and using a bungee cord, I locked the wheel in position—a poor man's autopilot. Robert Dean and I were expecting to eat fish all weekend, but then I remembered the fruit. I found an apple, bit, reached for the cabinet above the stove, and retrieved a protein bar. To think that nuts mixing with chocolate, coagulated together using unknown chemicals, could be so rejuvenating seemed absurd, so I brought another one with me and sped out to the stern.

Outside, Three Bands hung on like a crab to a piling. At nearly seven knots, it might have been the fastest the wind had ever hit his face. "Unbelievable," I mumbled.

I waved the granola protein bar in the air to entice him back like I'd done to Scupper and bit the bar again.

At twenty feet away, he gripped the sides of the canoe with a fearful face, a deep concern in his eye, clamping onto the canoe as though it was speeding a hundred miles an hour. His arms, skinny, flexed and thin, but defined muscles revealed along narrow bone. Black hair tied up in a ponytail, now came loose as individual strands frizzled in chaos, crossing over his eyes.

I made one last attempt to connect. "It's good. You'll like it," and tossed the wrapped protein bar into the canoe and went back up to the helm.

Once we arrived at the mouth of the creek, I briefed myself with possible action plans upon arriving back to camp. Getting in and getting out was my main focus—*with* Robert Dean.

I wanted to bring Chief the cobia fillets, and after seeing his satisfied face, head straight back to the skiff, un-foul the propeller, and get the hell out of there and back to Sara and Scupper. I said to myself with confidence and fortitude, "In and out ... in and out ... no problem." After repeating it a few more times, I began to believe that self-motivation was only a thing sad people did.

I lowered the bulky houseboat to an easy idle and slugged to the stern deck, where Three Bands sat still in the canoe, sorrowful and disconnected.

From the Cutoff's main bay, numerous finger creeks snaked in every direction, and were loaded with tight switchbacks that concealed several hidden pockets of water. Straight ahead lay the creek that would carry us back to the camp—and to Robert Dean and my skiff. But it was a tight run, and with a vessel in tow, threading it clean would be anything but easy.

Three Bands gripping the sides of the canoe reminded me of a child sitting on a coin-operated riding machine propped outside an old grocery store. Since the granola protein bar didn't do the trick, I tried another tactic to lure this off-the-grid maniac back to the boat.

I ascended the metal ladder leading to the roof deck, brought my hand flat to my eyebrow, to block the sun. I wanted to show him how far I could see from up so high and panned my head, sweeping the mangroves tips and pointing. My gestures couldn't have been made any clearer, but he still sat stubborn.

I whispered, "What is your problem…?"

Pondering the next move, I climbed back down, found the cooler, reached for a beer, chugged it down like it was the last one on Earth, then popped another top, and skipped back to the stern deck.

Dehydration on an empty stomach, and the minimal volume of alcohol in one beer facilitated a slight buzz. And to make a bolder move, I swiped the stern rope into my grasp that I'd tied to the canoe wedged behind an exposed stringer and pulled.

Three Bands paddled in a rebellious manner, rowing backward—saw my action as threatening.

I again pulled on the rope, taking up slack into the houseboat.

Again, Three Bands back paddled, tightening the rope.

With the sun's position at its current angle, introduced an over-hung mangrove limb, setting the canoe in the sun and the houseboat in the shade, which bumped a pair of fresh pilings I had never seen before. "Hmm. Don't remember these being here." I eyed the pilings that stuck three feet out of the water.

"Unaababa … unaababa," he said again.

I turned back to Three Bands. "What does that mean?"

Each lap of rope I wrapped around the deck chock stymied the ineffectual backward progress he desperately tried to accomplish—but he continued regardless. And once he came within ten feet, he relented, submitting in defeat, slamming the paddle hard onto the bow.

Using my free hand, I held the cold beer, discharged the contents by way of a long gulp, then shook him the empty can. "Beer," I said, letting out a strident burp.

Frustrated, and no longer intimidated by this man, I drew in the last few feet of slack, bumping his canoe's bow on the outboard engine. In the cabin, I fetched another two beers, cracked open the first can, and left the second on the fillet table in front of him—then sipped again as his mental wheels turned.

"There's one right here for you. Come and get it."

He reached for the granola bar and bit at the wrapper.

I extended my hand. "Here … give it."

He blinked, leaped to the bow of his canoe, climbed over the stern taffrail, and handed me the granola bar. I ripped it open, tossed it back to him, and drank more beer. He bit the bar and chewed from the side cautiously, like a lion chewing down a buffalo's leg bone. His teeth were deep yellow, covered in layers of plaque—sheered to points, which had probably been sharpened from a steady diet of shellfish. He kept his head down while finishing the offering.

I decided to test our trust and handed him a beer. He accepted, shook the can, and placed it to his ear, listening to the building carbonation. I let out a temperate smile, didn't want to spook him and nullify our progress.

"No no. No shake," I said, and unclamped the beer from his bony hand.

Old habits die hard, so I tapped on the top of the can to soften the carbonating build-up, and in front of him eased it open. He flinched from the sound of the carbonation leaving the can.

I said, trying to hold back a laugh, "Don't worry, it won't hurt you."

His reaction to my grinning said he might be open to jokes, seemed to understand my half-smile as a kind of truths. He accepted the can from my hand, took a sip, then another, reacting like that of a child tasting something for the first time. He drank again.

Pointing to my chest, "Shamus," I said.

He focused on my chest.

I repeated, "Shamus."

For his own reasons, he wasn't biting, remained reserved, keeping himself shut tighter than an oyster in red tide. Wouldn't allow himself to connect even after our joking. I did, though, feel we'd gained a sliver of trust between the two of us, but him avoiding eye contact while sipping the beer told me he wasn't ready and fought to repress the ground we'd gained.

Now that I'd lashed the canoe tight to the stern chock, I geared the houseboat, and the outboard pushed us ahead.

*****

I hadn't intended to bypass the turn which led to my skiff, but Three Bands insisted we proceed another way, opposite my skiff. "Koota atta," he kept repeating, and pointing. My lone move was to give in as I assumed we'd arrive at the bank where the food was being prepared. It made sense to dock us at the most convenient place—no sense in trudging through the mangrove thicket.

Our arrival at the loading docks didn't go unnoticed. A younger crowd had spotted us motoring in from quite a way down the manmade canal. Kids by the bunch waited anxiously as the houseboat chugged down the canal.

We pulled in, and I beached the houseboat on a twenty-foot section of sandy bank between two mangrove bushes. Busy women occupied the fillet tables, and the stone-surrounded fires flicked hot embers into the sky.

Three Bands leapt over the railing, dismounting from the front bow, no doubt to impress, but caught a leg on the edge of the metal railing and dove headfirst into the sand.

"Lightweight," I mumbled.

The gathered children busted into laughter, while the adults remained obediently silent.

Now that we'd made little progress, I wondered if he'd keep on the same path to trustworthiness, or now that he was back in camp, and seen again as a warrior leader, he'd digress our developing friendship.

The early teens seemed to be curious about the strange vessel that had just pulled into their home port; the cynical adults protested, wearing skeptical and cautious expressions. The Moms had to hold back many of the younger kids that were eager to join in the investigation.

At the stern, I reached for the fish cooler, then feeling its weight, decided on obtaining a hand.

Wondering where Robert Dean might be, I motioned at Three Bands, who was accompanied by his inferior group of fellows, to follow me. He understood and said something to a small boy in the group. I then led the kid to the cooler and pointed to one end. I lifted to simulate the weight. He didn't bother to discuss, but grinned understandingly, then called out, "*Kitu.*"

I thought, *Kitu?*

Within a few seconds, the smallest kid in the group stomped onto the bow, and slipped to the cooler. His face was young and curious. He wore one red band on a skinny, tan arm, signifying a lower rank; face was plain, and a bandana made from unknown material held in place long, dark, horse-straight hair. He wore a necklace made from what looked like shell, like mine, dangling around his neck. He had bare feet and one of his middle toes was gone.

Three Bands pointed to the cooler and the kid lifted the opposite end.

I returned the smile. "Nice."

Kitu visually pored over the houseboat's exterior as he carried the fish cooler along it. I led him off the stern and through the main cabin. He nearly dropped the cooler in distraction, fixating on the helm station. Three Bands barked an order and the kid continued in silence.

The melting ice sloshed as we offloaded the cooler. I dropped my end on the short beach next to the houseboat and pawed at my back—just from the short carry off the boat it throbbed. I bore a painful, intentional grimace across my face. Three Bands noticed and called to another young male.

"Kinu," he said.

Another exuberant young kid came before us and lifted the other end of the cooler and together the kids transported it into the bush.

Once we popped through the first trailhead leading away from the beach, I noticed Three bands had set men to guard the houseboat.

We continued as they led me down the wall of shells, through the short path toward the community's nucleus, to Chief's dwelling.

*****

Our strenuous walk to Chief's residence wasn't the spectacle it had been earlier. Unlike the first time, they'd called no villagers, nothing ceremonious, and no serenading children.

I followed without command, no spear pressing my back—only the shuffle of men moving through the palmettos. For a moment, I could almost have been one of them.

After a few mysterious stares from villagers, we reached the imposing entrance leading to the vestibule of the Chief's mansion, where Chief had returned to his elevated chair, and his wife, wearing the bald eagle hair band, sat beside him in a lower set chair.

Kinu and Kitu placed the cooler near the base of their leader's chair and vanished from sight.

I wasn't sure if food was so sparse that the presentation had to be done in secrecy, or if it wasn't such a big deal, the others needn't be disturbed from their chores.

They arranged me facing the Chief, and after no sign of Robert Dean, I began to feel anxious. Last I saw him they'd separated us, carrying him limply down an unknown path.

Three Bands remained next to his boss's chair, saying something in a low register that I couldn't hear. Their causerie continued for a few seconds more before my nerves claimed the best of me.

"Where is my—?" I raised my hand, holding it out at the same height as my head, like measuring a person standing next to me. "…friend?"

Three Bands' jaw bite tightened.

I noticed and repeated, "My friend? Where is he?"

Chief's wife seemed to understand my words as I eyed her. Her deep brown eyes rotated toward her husband's stoic face.

A bead of sweat formed at his temple while his intimidating stare locked on me. We were having another staring contest. I sensed the wheels grinding in his mind. After a few excruciating minutes, he pointed toward the cooler. Three Bands bent down and opened it. Chief's curiosity overwhelmed him, and he leaned forward, enough to see the entirely of its contents.

Three Bands reached in and lifted out the tail of the cobia, presenting it high like a newborn baby. White-fleshed meat and thick black skin of the fish caught Chief's eyes. Three Bands returned the tail to the cooler and lifted out the cobia's head and presented it the same.

His wife cracked a slight grin and turned her attention toward Chief, awaiting a response. All I could do was observe while an inborn feeling told me that if Chief wasn't to be wholly satisfied with our offerings, Robert Dean and I would find our way back to the stone of death.

Finaly, his reaction to the cobia's head was what I had hoped for. He shifted slightly in his seat and cracked a barely noticeable grin.

Feeling brave, I went a step farther and reached into the cooler myself and pulled out a bag of fruit—mangos, apples, and grapefruit. He motioned me forward.

I handed him the bag, and regarding the plastic, his eyebrow went ridged, forehead furling.

Lavish juice dripped as I bit into the mango. He observed, perhaps to see if I would fall ill. After I chewed and swallowed, I handed him a mango.

He bit—eyes widened while the sweet nectar sequestered his taste buds. He finished chewing on rotted teeth and handed the bag to his wife. She inspected the contents for herself.

Chief's hands raised, swiping the air, not in a cross pattern, but rotated in a similar way that his wife had done while blessing me before heading to the houseboat. His eyes rested shut. After a wordless minute, his eyes opened. Three Bands eased back to his side—they conversed again—and shortly after, a verdict was in.

Three Bands slipped away, and following a long, silent minute, Robert Dean's deep unmistakable voice entered the area.

"I'm goin', I'm goin', no need to get pushy." They brought him out from behind the Chief's chair and our eyes met, then we grinned. Sweat had soaked through his jean suspenders. His white T-shirt was stained brown under his armpits. A salt ring had formed at the base of his white hat, and his boot laces were loose and untied. I finally could breathe a sigh of relief.

"Glad yah came back for me," he said, sliding in next to me.

"I actually came back for the skiff." I reached out for a handshake. "How you feeling?"

"Good, good," he said raising his chin, rubbing his stomach, "I had a feast of oysters and mullet."

I inspected him from head to toe. "Good, I'm glad."

Sitting, Chief studied the two of us conversing, letting us have our moment. Three Bands hung alongside in patience, a well-practiced trait.

"I see you brought the cooler," Robert Dean said. "Cobia?" He peeked at Chief and pointed his thumb. "He ain't goin' kill us now is he … now that we've given him dinner?"

"That's the idea. But I'm not so sure we're out of the woods just yet."

Robert Dean glanced around. "These people ain't so bad it seems. That is … if they don't want to kill yah."

"You get any liquids? What did you drink?"

"They brought me awn back to some kind of medical hut. A grey-haired, short woman let me suckle from her nipple—"

I paused. "Say what?"

He sniffed his arms. "Kidding. I'm not sure what it was, tasted like rainwater ... did the ol' job though. I feel much better."

"Good good."

He yawned. "I passed out for a little while, I think. How long were yah gone?"

I glanced at my muck-covered watch, then wiped off the face using my thumb. "I'm not sure, looks like my watch is dead."

"Dead?"

"Yup," I answered, looking at the screen.

"Interestin'..."

"Interesting?"

"Yeah. Kinda strange, don't you think?"

"What? That my watch is dead?"

"Yeah, kinda convenient," he said.

"It is, isn't it..."

Robert Dean grinned.

I said, "It's been an hour or two ... maybe more."

Our reunion was over, and Chief signaled Three Bands to lead us from the mansion.

Cool air of dawn whirled across my face while the sun dimmed as I stepped out into the open. The village's activity had increased—people were pouring toward the general direction of the creek bank where the houseboat sat afloat, as well as the fish prepping area. I was no genius, but it seemed it might be time for dinner.

Robert Dean and I abided and waited for instructions from Three Bands, but he'd vanished from sight.

I glanced around. "Did you see where he went?"

"Who? The tall guy wearing the three armbands?"

"Yeah, it's strange that he just took off and left us."

His eyebrows raised. "Maybe we've been set free?"

"I wish, but that's what I meant by *we're not* out of the woods just yet."

Robert Dean looked me in the eye. "What do you mean, *yet?*"

Still standing in the doorway to Chief's mansion, I turned to my friend. "While you were taking a snooze, me and that dude … paddled all the way to the houseboat, and instead of paddling all the way back, I brought the—"

Robert Dean leaned back. "You didn't…"

I jerked up my hand. "Hang on a second."

His lips pressed against his teeth. "Shamus, now they know about it!"

"I know, I know. But all we had was a tiny wooden canoe. There was no way the cooler and all the tools I needed to fix the skiff's prop were going to fit. Plus, the wind picked up, and it just wasn't worth it. I mean, they would have found it anyway…"

Okay, good." He began to nod as though it was good news now. "So, let's get on out to it and haul butt!"

"That's the thing … I think it's being guarded."

He shook his head. "Oh, man, we're screwed now. You've really done it."

"Chill." I placed a hand onto his moist shoulder. "I think if we play our cards right, we'll be fine."

"I *doubt* that."

"If we just chill out and go with the flow for a little while, and when the moment is right, we jet." I held up my thumb. "Cool?"

"I don't think we've got a choice, now do we?" Robert Dean's tone was portentous. I could tell when he wasn't kidding around. He wanted out of here, no denying that.

I peeked along the pathways. "I'm not sure why Three Bands left, but it can't be good."

My friend's forehead wrinkled. Skepticism set in; judgement followed. "Three Bands?" he asked. "You know his name?"

"It's just what I've been calling him."

"That guy is a mean son-of-a-bitch, I'll tell yah. He doesn't seem to be none too friendly. Did you see the way he treated us earlier? Like we were animals."

"They were just being cautious is all, after our failed escape. I mean, you were taken care of, no?"

"I guess…"

We both stood dumbfounded as to what to do next.

A few conspicuous females returned through the path leading to the houseboat, each carried a palm frond-woven basket.

"I gave him a beer," I finally said, eyes slanted.

"Gave *whom* a beer?"

"Three Bands."

Robert Dead stomped his feet in anger. "You gave that dirty, smelly, homeless man a beer? One of our *dang* beers!"

"Yeah, he liked it—drank a few."

"My God, Shamus, you're *killin'* me here."

"Don't worry." I winked. "I didn't show him the apple pie."

As soon as the words left my lips, a smile materialized on Robert Dean's face. My friend was a hard worker, day in and day out, repairing septic tanks—not a job for those with a weak stomach. He didn't like anyone messing with his vice.

A devious smirk crossed over his face. "Oh, yeah? That's on the houseboat still?" He knew it was, as his eyes darted in thought.

"Don't even think about it, please. Not yet, at least."

"Why not? I'm just goin' mosey on up and sneak on. They'll never know I'm there."

"At two-hundred-plus pounds and feet the size of snowshoes, you wouldn't make it within fifty feet before someone noticed."

"Really?"

"It's guarded." This was a deter tactic that I knew was frivolous.

"Oh…" His face squinted. "I'm not going in the daylight … more like sneak at night sometime—when all these reality-impaired gypsies are sleepin'."

"You won't make it."

"And why not?" he asked, in amusement.

I said from the corner of my mouth, "Not with your loud, forward stomping, heavy-footed swagger you won't."

He mumbled, "Better than your slow, draggin' foot, turkey trottin'—"

"What was that?" I interrupted.

"Nothin'," he said.

"Do whatever you think is necessary, but remember one thing…"

Robert Dean stuck his jaw forward, "And what would that be?"

"Remember that little sacrificial death ceremony earlier?"

"Oh, that…"

"The stone of death ring a bell?"

"Uh-huh."

"Remember how…" I paused and air-quoted: "…how cold it was while Black Mask stood ready and willing to slice off your noggin and use it for a soccer ball?"

"Oh, that was just their own way of puttin' a scare in us, undastand?"

"Well, did it work?"

"Kinda."

We remained together, standing dubious in the middle of a primitive society, which I concluded existed undetected at the north end of The Myakka Cutoff—without outside influence—for an unknown amount of time.

Robert Dean removed a rag from his pocket, lifted off his hat, wiped his forehead, and returned the handkerchief to his right overalls pocket.

I too adjusted, removing my visor, then sunglasses, wiping them clean. Then returned them to my pocket, and my visor atop my head.

Robert Dean broke the reflective silence, asking, "Now what?"

I shrugged, said, "Now we eat."

Chapter Ten

"What do we have here?" my friend asked as we arrived at the bank, where the fish-cleaning stations stood in neat, systematic rows.

Bountiful holdings with endless assortments of seafood scattered in depth on all five tables. Of the five makeshift wooden tables, two amassed in staggered, tippy piles of hearty chunks of fish fillets with intact fish heads. A hodge-podge of shellfish—mainly oysters and conch shells stacked up another two tables. Large mounds of unidentifiable meat overflowed the last table.

I noticed three female villagers choosing from the mishmash of fresh catch, placing their preferred fish into identical palm frond-woven baskets, and finished, walked off silently.

"Looks like some kind of buffet, or somethin' like it," Robert Dean said.

"I'd say you're correct."

We eased toward the tables to avoid contact, observing like picking our sides at the local deli. On the first few tables, the species identification was clear. While assessing visually, I put the snook and redfish at forty-plus-inches. The fringe reeked of brine and fish slime. Neat stacks of Snapper and mullet of every size glistened with seawater, scales catching the dimming light. Piles of whole pinfish, grunts, and sand brim scattered like spilled treasure. Flies hovered in buzzing clouds, gulls cried overhead as the Cutoff's finest lay at our fingertips—gleaming and ready to cook.

Robert Dean observed in awe, commenting, "Unbelievable."

"I know, right? Never seen so much fish at one time— illegal fish."

My friend led us to the last table where two massive chunks of gray skin, pinkish white meat covered the entirety of the wooden table. I held a piece in my hand and rolled it between my index finger and thumb, suspicious of its texture. If what my fingers told me was true, it seemed that these villagers had caught, killed, and carved up a dolphin.

I turned to my friend. "I think these people are eating dolphin, look." I pointed to the soggy, thin, gray-skinned meaty chunk.

Robert Dean scoped the area, knelt, inspecting the contents under the table. "Not dolphin—look again."

Underneath the table, a head layered in scattered sand and shell bits faced me. It had clear features like a distinctive pudgy face, snout full of whiskers, and two round definitive breathing holes. There was no mistaking what kind of meat it was. Under the table, resting on its side, though rolled into place, was the head of a manatee with tiny, white, dead eyes.

My friend and I faced each other in shock. He said, "Man, somebody will be in big trouble if word of this gets out."

My expression turned questionable. "Gets out?"

"Yeah, yah know..." My friend clicked his cheeks, "...when we skedaddle—"

I shook my head. "I'm not sure running to the cops when we get out of here is the best thing to do."

He nodded understandingly. "No rat ... I get it."

"Well," I said, crossing my arms. " I'm not."

"I don't know about you," my friends said, licking his chapping lips, "but I'm takin' a gigantic snook fillet."

"Really?"

"Yup, I've yet to eat snook. All these years comin' on down here to sunny Florida." He pointed at me. "You've never put me on a keeper snook—"

"I've put you on plenty of keeper snook."

He swiped his hands into a measuring position. "Legal snook. *Leeegal.*" Robert Dean reached in and selected a snook fillet the size of an adult sneaker. He held it up proudly. "Here's a nice one."

I peeked around, didn't see any grills. "Where are you going to cook that? I doubt sneaking on the houseboat and firing up the camping grill is an option right now."

His eyes spun to the immediate area, cheeks puffed, his attention settling on a smoldering fire pit dug twenty yards away. "Right over there," he said, nudging his chin.

Around the firelit pit, hot embers drifted upward, holding, then raining down on the hefty piles of shells they'd stacked in deliberate patterns that traced its circumference. Four other fire pits remained fireless but showed definite signs of use—dark char marks surrounding the neat alignment of perimeter stones. Robert Dean found a stick and began to stoke our pit.

I glanced around. "Are you just gonna to lay it down in the fire? Might need a pan or something."

Seeing Robert Dean's hearty choice of snook fillet, I imagined its taste. Just the thought made my stomach's digestive acids bubble like hungry baby birds—mouths open, waiting to snatch a freshly chewed chunk. For now, I went along with the plan.

"Looks like we can get her fired back up in no time," my friend said.

Three female villagers walked past, watching and giggling. My attention drew back to the fish tables where a short woman, holding a small child, began to select her fish. She lowered the child to the ground, sliced off a chunk the size of a paperback book and tucked it into a satchel. She then lifted the child back under her arm. Over her mom's shoulder, the toddler found me with her eyes. Her dark, tanned skin blended among the pits of deep-blue child eyes. Long, straight, black hair flowed overtop her shoulders and down her back. At me, she tilted her head, producing one of the most innocent smiles I'd ever seen. I made a funny face, puffing my cheeks out as I held in air. She giggled like a shy child should, tucking her face into the shoulder of Mom. Tiny feet wiggled, brushing them against Mom's Spanish moss, Hawaiian-style skirt. Her head popped out and taunted again, enticing me to play. The moment felt incredibly real. I could have been in line at a grocery store doing the same routine.

Fire coals glowed while the fire began to perk, and by the minute, Robert Dean's confidence increased. He peeped— attention found the houseboat floating down the bank. "I know where there's perfect cooking utensils alright..."

The houseboat floated about fifty yards down the bank, and from where I sat, six or seven men ringed the vessel, spears leveled, ready for action.

"You don't see those men surrounding it?" I nodded to it. "There's even a man in a canoe afloat, watching the stern."

"I see 'em alright."

"If I were you, I'd just relax and—"

His head signaled toward the center of the village. "I bet they're guardin' from them, not us."

This point flagged as pertinent to our current situation. If the assumption of Robert Dean that those villagers were protecting our houseboat from their own people, not us, proved to be correct, then who's to prevent us from walking down there, boarding up, and shoving off?

I side-eyed for eavesdroppers toward the shell wall, the path back to the center of the village, and now with decreasing visibility, resembled a villager-haunted tunnel vacant of all activity. I then glanced down the manmade canal leading up to the houseboat. The setting sun had reduced the men guarding it to black silhouettes.

"Are they staying all night?" I muttered—then said, "Why do you think they're guarding against themselves?"

"Who knows, Shamus. All I'm sayin' is that I'm hungry and we need to cook this fish before I drop dead."

I elbowed toward the houseboat. "Okay, then go for it…"

"You ain't comin' with me?"

Swatting at the no-see-ums, I told him, "I'm coming alright, just to keep *you* in check."

We both hit the sandy bank and began pacing to the houseboat, but not before Robert Dean temporarily rested the snook fillet on the edge of a stone protruding from the fire pit. Just when we found a comfortable pace, out from the shadows thumped Three Bands. Ahead of us, he snuck through an undisclosed trail, blocking our path.

"Here we go again," my friend said from the corner of his mouth.

"Just be cool. I think we had a breakthrough while out fetching the cobia."

"Speaking of cobia … how come we ain't getting none of it?" His voice trailed

off, then added, "I *caught* the flippin' thing."

Three Bands swept up, wearing the same intense expression, but this time he wasn't alone. A little boy stood behind him, hugging his right leg. *His son*, I thought. He signaled us to follow him—we did.

"Looks like he didn't bring his spear this time," Robert Dean noted.

I said nothing as he led us toward the creepily dark path toward the center of the camp where the mansion sat, and Chief.

Robert Dean saw it, too. "Oh shit. Not this place again…"

Three Bands spun halfway to face us, seemed to understand the comment. He wore a type of thin, leathery shirt, probably made from animal hide. Across his back, someone had painted small drawings of winged birds on the long-deadened skin. One looked like an eagle; another resembled an osprey—all painted using a kind of red, inky dye— basic, simple drawings. Obviously, his son was the artist.

We neared the entrance to the chief's mansion, but we abruptly passed it by, and—under Three Bands's guidance, we set off toward the village's northern rim. Robert Dean and I labored to keep up. Our tour guide paced through the shells and sugar sand as though on wheels. Even the small child easily kept up.

After another half mile, the trail bent into a secluded corner where four petite huts stood in a tidy row. Each wore a roof of thatched palm fronds, their frames cleaved from sun-bleached pine, where every one mirrored of the next. They were the same clustered dwellings we'd passed on the way in— unchanged, as though they'd been waiting for us.

Three Bands guided us past a glowing fire pit and to the front entrance of one of the huts. He pointed to a small bowl and satchel resting on the scuffed doorstep, then held his hands out as if he were a maître d' showing us to our rooms.

Robert Dean and I strolled into the darkness of the hut, where only light from the moon beamed in from a break in an overhead slash pine.

Three Bands and the child slipped back onto the path, their outlines thinning until they seemed to dissolve into the night itself.

Robert Dean spun toward the eerie bush. "He didn't stay long, huh?"

"No, he didn't," I said, noticing the adjacent hut, where another group were sitting on tree stumps, eating around a private fire pit. "Hey, look at them," I whispered behind me.

No answer.

"Robert Dean?" I checked inside the hut. "Where did you go?" I whispered intently.

With him nowhere in sight, and suspicion stirring, I returned to the moonlit trailhead and peered down the path. The air was lighter, cooler away from the heat of the fire. Now wasn't the time to vanish or play games. I stepped off the trail and jogged back to the doorway. "Robert Dean!"

"Back here," he blurted. "Quiet…"

His voice emitted from behind the hut, and as I took steps in the voice's direction, moonlight sparkle glistened off my friend's shiny boot tip.

"What are you doing back—never mind."

"Hang on, bub," he said. "I wouldn't come back here right now."

Shaking my head in the dark, I said turning away, "Nice … just perfect. What happened to the creepy crawlies?"

I didn't wait for an answer. Back to the fire pit I moseyed, which sat fifteen feet from the entrance to the hut. Shells and rocks surrounded the warm fire, forming a border to contain the flames. I sat down and rubbed my hands together as though to perform a magic trick. The flame burned bright, sending small embers snapping into the night, each riding a faint whistle as the wood exhaled.

I sat waiting for my friend when I noticed an odd-looking stone in our fire, about the size of a loaf of bread, set at the edge of the searing coals. I glanced in peripheral toward the other campsite, and toward two people sitting on a stumped bench facing my direction. A man stoked the fire, and the other, a woman, sat somber-faced—a couple. He noticed me peeping and stood.

"Dammit," I mumbled.

Using a tool similar to a wooden spatula, the man reached forward and removed a chunk of meat from the flame of his fire. His block resembled the same stone resting in our fire— then I remembered the satchel.

At the doorway, I carried the satchel and bowl to the fire. Some of the liquid sloshed from the clay bowl along the way, leaving it only half-full. Settling again on the stump, I unwrapped the still-green palm frond and revealed its contents. Robert Dean then emerged back from around the hut.

"I would not go back there if I was you!".

"I hope you washed your hands."

"Sure did, bub." He sat and eyed me holding the satchel. "What is in that thing anyway?"

"Food," I said.

His brows raised. "Oh, yeah…?"

I hefted a thick, weighty slab of what might've been snook—or something pretending to be—and held it over the fire. The heat warmed at my knuckles, the skin of the fish glistening in the light. "Looks like it. Yup." I scanned the fire pit for an area ideal to begin cooking. "What are we gonna use as a cooking platform, or are you thinkin' snook kabob?"

Robert Dean didn't answer, so using my hands, I wiped the fish clean the best I could—eliminating the slime, scales, and elemental debris.

"Guess this will have to do," I said, and laid the snook down flat on the slab of rock resting on the orange-hot bed of coals. An immediate sizzle of burning flesh revealed the rock's increasing temperature. Robert Dean heard it.

"That must be limestone," my friend said.

"Limestone?"

"Has to be," he answered.

"Why does it have to be?"

He settled onto his stump. "Well, for this area, I'm surprised people don't cook with it more often ... limestone and what-not."

I agreed. Limestone, a carbon-based rock, formed in warm, shallow water. When all the miniature sea creatures, which had lived millions of years ago, died, they sank to the bottom and their bodies built up on the seafloor. Limestone was more or less the fossilized and calcified bits and pieces of those creatures.

I said, "Didn't think Florida limestone would make such a good cooking tool."

"Well, these small chunks here..." He reached for a small stick and poked the block. "...will work for a few dozen cooks but will eventually crack and break apart from bein' heated up then cooled over and over again. Up north yah can find the good, dense stuff, if you're so lucky."

Sometimes I forget how Robert Dean's brain works. When sober, his recall ability is quite impressive.

We sat in silence for a few relaxing minutes, staring off into the fire, monitoring the two-inch-thick snook fillet turn flaky and white.

"Forget about turnin' her," Robert Dean said as I made motions to do so. "Just cook it on one side,"

"If it burns, it's your ass," I said. "One thing I've realized throughout the years is that there's only one true way to ruin fish, and that is to overcook it."

He coughed, and grinned. "Anything else in that leaf basket?"

"Not sure." I reached in. "Interesting..."

"What?"

"Seems to be cattails in here."

"Cattails?"

"Sure is, here." I handed them over.

He laid the green pouch onto the shells surrounding the fire. "I think I'll just stick to the fish for now."

As we sat, and our fish sizzled, I shut my eyes, imagining all the similarities of lounging about in any campground in Florida—but with one single difference: it was incredibly quiet, not an ambient sound except the occasional crackle of burning wood and searing flesh.

Robert Dean yawned and I followed.

I said, "I guess we're staying the night, huh?"

My friend began to fidget, mind working, glancing out toward the dark trail toward the adjoining camp, where the man and woman sat and ate dinner. He sat still for a minute, ill at ease.

"No escaping, man," I said, to stoke his internal fire. "Remember?"

He checked the darkness of the trail. "I'm not goin' anywhere, but right now I bet we could run for it."

"I'm sure that's the case, but I've gotta un-foul the prop before we can *actually* get out of here,"

"Could take the houseboat..."

"Houseboat is slow and antiquated." I paused and waited for a reaction, then when his mouth opened to respond, "Plus, it's being guarded."

"I'm sure it moves mighty faster than what these dirt lovers can paddle."

I thought back to earlier on when Three Bands had gripped the sides of the canoe, freaked out at a measly seven knots. "You might be right, but I'm not leaving the skiff." I shook my head. "Not going to happen."

"I know yah won't. That's why I'm goin' give this place one more day … hell, maybe I'll learn somethin'."

I countered with, "Or maybe you could teach them something?"

"Teach them something?" he asked. "What am I suppose teach *these people?*"

"Well, by your choice of bathrooms…" I signaled toward the back of the hut. "By the looks of things around here, maybe they could use some tips."

"Naaah," he replied, reaching for the wooden spork I removed from the satchel, laying it on the shells. "In my eyes, the whole goal of waste disposal is to bury it deep, let the earth absorb it. They seem to have that figured out quite alright."

"Is it ready?" I asked.

Robert Dean leaned in to assess the tenderness of the fish. He punctured the meat using the spork. Since the utensil slipped easily through the flesh, he seemed satisfied and cut a sample, brought it up to his mouth, then stopped, blew to cool, and stopped again.

I observed. "Go ahead, don't be scared."

"Ha! Scared—me?"

"I'm just saying…" I grinned. "Don't quit on me now. You go ahead and eat that right now."

"Why? So you can see if I drop dead?"

"I know how bad you need meat…"

"Funny." He held the fish to his chin.

"Just think, if you do die, and I manage to escape, I'll brand you as a hero. I'll say you stopped a speeding spear by leaping in front of it. You risked your life to save mine. How's that sound?"

Before I could finish, Robert Dean bit down.

I couldn't hold back while he chewed. "Good?"

He continued chewing, replied, "It's delicious."

"I figured it would be. Kinda hard to mess up snook."

"Could use some hot sauce, though," he added.

Robert Dean handed me the spork, and I plucked a chunk, ate it, and reached for the clay bowl resting on the ground beside me. I suspiciously held the half-empty bowl up to the fire.

"It's rainwater—gua-ran-teed," my friend said.

"How do you know?"

"Look around, Shamus—it sure as hell ain't *Perrier*."

I rotated the bowl like panning for gold. "It could be anything."

"Don't be sacred."

"I was just looking for bugs."

"Curse these things." Robert Dean faced me intently, swatting no-see-ums while awaiting my findings on the purity of the water.

I leaned the bowl toward the light. "Looks clean."

He said, "I knew it was rainwater because that's the same kinda bowl I drank from earlier when I was feelin' none too well."

We both finished up the stone-cooked snook and headed into the hut. While nearing pitch dark, a single, circular moonbeam shone onto the dirt floor.

"I can't see a friggin' thing," my friend said.

I told him, "Me either, hang on." I went outside and snatched a burning stick from the fire and brought it into the hut. The torch worked well enough to see two sleeping mats. There were no windows, but a small circular sunroof. No shelves or anything. It was very plain.

"Careful with the flame, Shamus. This place will go up faster than a box of fireworks at a rodeo."

"No doubt, no doubt." I wafted the torch around to get a feel for the place. "Well, at least we don't have to share a bed."

Robert Dean chose a plump mat and plopped down. "What's this mattress made from?" Something annoying was poking his ribs. He pulled out the contents of a small hole. "Looks like more cattails."

I waved the torch at the door and then brought it back to the fire pit. There was movement out the corner of my eye. Our neighbors were also stepping into their hut. The man pressed on her back, leading the woman in. I went back into our hut.

Robert Dean stretched hard, rustling the cattails. "Well, I guess the snook was okay. I'm not dead, *yet.*"

I laid down on my back and faced up at the darkness of the hut. "No, you're not, but if the snook won't kill us, the no-see-ums will."

Chapter Eleven

Morning arrived though my eyes had never closed. The hush of an early night had morphed into a full-blown orchestra of Florida's nocturnal all-stars. Owls hooted, insects buzzed, crickets carried on like they were warning the Gods. And Robert Dean's snoring, a log-sawing solo that rattled through the thin air. Not to mention the cattail-filled hide bags on which we lay, rustling after every delicate movement.

Awaking in an unfamiliar place comes with an initial shock—a morning recap that required a pithy reflective moment. I reviewed the previous day's events, analyzed, and set forth a plan. My first breath of morning air—cool, crisp, and clean—felt like a tonic, a reminder of why one emerges into the wild in the first place. The notion of rolling over for another hour's sleep never even crossed my mind; the day had already claimed me.

This time though, no warm body to curl next to, no warm shower to jump into, no freshly squeezed mango juice, no anything—which reminded me of Sara.

At this time, Sara would also be waking. Her perfect symmetrical face, eyes puffed from sleep—strands of golden blonde hair crossing, overlapping, and frizzing as she leaned close for a morning kiss. Sara had the type of face that required no need for makeup. Inadequacies didn't compromise her complexion, and she knew it. Seeing her unaltered, full lips, petite nose, and eyes blue as a jay's wing in the morning gave me joy. She had a habit of talking in her sleep when she'd had too much wine. She claimed she didn't, but I'd noticed it on many occasions. She always told me, "Why not record me, then?" I never could.

On normal days, Scupper was the first one up. A remarkable dog in the respect that she knew when to make noise, and when to stay silent. When morning arrived, she'd wait patiently until the first signs of movement before letting out a single peep; her tail slapping the laminated floor, head resting on the corner of the air mattress—watching and waiting.

*****

After my recap, I rose. Even without a working watch, the time was easy to judge. By the season's date and the gray-blue light of morning, I guessed it to be around seven o'clock.

I wobbled at first, staggering to the doorway, leaning against the unsound framed threshold, and gathered my bearings. The recently deceased fire no longer blazed. Its inner ring had burned, charred, and seemed larger during the shadows of darkness.

The air, if I were to guess, was approaching seventy-five degrees with a low dew point, typical Florida morning this time of year. I exited the hut.

Down the path, groups of short figures—mostly women—moved toward the center, lending the scene a touch of normalcy. I glanced around, and, with no idea what else to do, drifted back into the hut.

On the homespun mattress, Robert Dean lay spread-eagle as if he were at home on the couch. Both of his overalls were unbuttoned over a shirtless chest, were a slight bush of hair sprouted between his pectorals.

"Get up," I said, kicking the corner where his head rested.

Motionless, he opened his eyes as though he was never asleep. "I'm awake."

Surprised, I asked, "How long have you been awake?"

"Not long, hour or so," he replied. "What's the plan?"

I headed back to the doorway. "Probably get the prop unfouled quick as possible and get the heck out of here."

"Sounds good." He threw his arms forward so his body would follow. Getting up, he took his shirt off the floor, waved it straight, put it on, then added, "I'ma get buckled up and see what's for breakfast."

"Breakfast?" I asked.

"No," he corrected. "Coffee."

I frowned. "You can't be serious."

"Sure as shit am. My gut's tellin' me it's breakfast … and coffee time."

"You *do* remember what's likely on the menu, right?"

"I do, but I'm goin' for the ol' houseboat."

"This again?" I said. "Guaranteed it's still being guarded."

"Well… We, shall, see."

"That we will," I said, and we left the hut and found the trail.

We didn't progress far. Out from the mist of early morning fog, Three Bands appeared as if gliding on ice, wearing the same three red bands tied around his left bicep. Today, he also wore makeshift flip-flops that looked professionally made, fashioned in a South American leather factory, but they weren't, and likely feigned from animal hide, since that seemed to be the overall theme. Unfortunately, the same tiny loincloth and spear had also made appearances.

He led us through the town as if we were wanted somewhere. We stopped multiple times so Three Bands could converse with other villagers with what I guessed to be sets of instructions. After the better part of an hour, we reached a breakfast table that held snook, redfish, manatee meat, and bits of mullet.

Youngsters stood guard over the food—designated flyswatters, who swatted anything that flew near it, including the dive-bombing horse flies.

"Not a bad idea," I mumbled. But this meat, at 8 o'clock in the morning, was incredibly unappealing, so I decided to skip.

Robert Dean took a quick gander at the smorgasbord and decided to also skip. "I'm not eating this," he said. "I mean look at it … besides from a few oysters and pinfish, all there is, is seafood! And that dang manatee head is still under the table!"

I said, "Was that not the plan, to eat fish all weekend?"

"Yes, but—"

"I'm right with you, not chancing it." I glanced down the beach at the houseboat, still under guard—just as we were.

Three Bands leaned over to us, appeared calm and collected, but patient. He used the spear to do the talking and waved it toward the plethora of meat and pointed a few yards away at the smoldering fire pit.

I gave him a "I'm not hungry" while pointing to my stomach, shaking my head, mouthing "N*ooo.*"

Robert Dean nudged my side and nodded toward the houseboat. Three Bands saw it but did nothing.

As we passed on the food, Three Bands grew irritated—couldn't seem to understand why we wouldn't dine. "*Mundua,*" he said. "*Mundua,*" he said again, lifting a piece of slime-coated fish to his mouth, simulating eating.

I said to him, "I'm okay."

Robert Dean ignored the warrior and focused on the houseboat as though he was about to break into a run. "Look, Shamus—they're raiding it," he squinted, "Yup … they sure are."

Down the bank, the boat was morphing into a source of great interest. A group of villagers had gathered at the water's edge, inching closer and closer. One person appeared to be on the bow deck.

"I think we're good for now," I said.

Once Three Bands realized that breakfast wasn't happening, he waved to start walking toward the houseboat. After passing the tables that held the fish, we went beyond the cleaning stations, where a dozen canoes aligned like cars in a parking lot.

The bank was narrow, at only fifteen feet from water to mangroves, which they had hacked back significantly—enough for a dead-on view if anyone snuck up the canal.

I nudged Robert Dean. "Look," I whispered toward a group of villagers protecting the houseboat.

"I see it. I see it."

Three Bands halted and signaled to the young male grasping the railing, straining to rock the houseboat, to de-board—he did, like a scolded child.

Robert Dean said, "Well, I think this is it. We're gettin' freed at last."

I wasn't convinced. "Eh … hold on."

Wearing the single armband, a younger male, who Three Bands called Kitu, and who'd helped with the cooler situation, rushed through the bush and slid to Three Bands' flank, clenching his fist tight. Strings of net material dangled from his hand. The boy wasn't out of breath but spoke fast using effort. He explained something to his leader, something that prompted a frown. Three Bands face contorted into an anger-filled frown as he turned to face us.

"Oh shit," Robert Dean said.

"Yup," I said. "I know what that is."

Robert Dean turned away, though afraid of it. "It's the netting from the prop. Oh. My. God."

Three Bands took the material and presented it to us, fingers tight, clamped to the palm fiber. Water dripped down his hand, across his wrist like a vein of clear liquid.

"I say we run for it," Robert Dean suggested, biting his knuckle.

"You first."

Three Bands said something to the kid, and he ran off. He then assumed the warrior persona, gripped his spear, and pointed us toward the trailhead leading in the direction of my skiff.

Just as we hit the trail, Three Bands' original team trudged free from the palmettos and fell in line with us. He returned his spear to my back but lacked the pressure of our first meeting. From behind, I heard Robert Dean speaking:

"Well, this couldn't be goin' aaany smoother."

I said, "We're being taken to the skiff, right? That was the plan."

"Yeah, but unless you got the tools hidden down your pants, I do believe we're not using our bare hands to remove any frickin props."

"Good point."

He suggested, "Why not ask your buddy here if you can go get them?"

I didn't answer but slowed my pace.

Robert Dean added, "Maybe drink a beer together…"

I stopped abruptly. "Very funny."

Three Bands opened his eyes wide, as though to send me a telepathic message. There was no threat from him, and I knew he didn't want—or need—to hurt us. For his benefit I contrived a small act. "Please, I need to go back to the boat." I pointed back toward the houseboat, which wasn't visible anymore.

The three subordinates focused on Three Bands, assessing his reaction. I knew that any sort of weakness shown at this crucial mentoring point determined his rank, so I laid it on thick.

Using hand signals, I simulated the use of a special tool, and that the propeller wouldn't come off without it, but with the excruciating language barrier, who knew what translated through and what didn't? I had no reason, at this point, to assume they knew anything about screwdrivers, or had even seen one, but I had to try.

His sidekicks then popped back and raised their spears.

My gaze fixed on Three Bands, willing some unspoken message across the space between us. His eyes flicked right to left, as if completing an inward measure of his own mood. Then with a sharp motion, he signaled us to turn, and we began marching toward the houseboat.

Soon as we were allowed back on the boat, it was Three Bands who joined us after he'd commanded the younger gang to wait on the bank.

Robert Dean wasted no time and went for the protein bars hidden above the sink. I went for the head.

Once out, I reached for the duffel bag, shouldering the preloaded tools. Three Bands eyed the cooler holding ice and beer.

I opened it and smiled. "Go for it."

Robert Dean noticed. "You goin' to let this guy drink *all our* beer?"

"If it keeps him on our good side, why not?"

"If you say so," he replied, eyeing Three Bands suspiciously, then winked. "You tossin' the apple pie in that bag, too?"

"Seriously?" I asked.

"Why not?"

"If these guys search this bag, you want them confiscating it?"

"Good point," he said, and reached for the bag of cannabis stowed in a small compartment under the helm. "I know what I'm taking." Once in hand, he snuck it inside a left overall pocket and patted it down. "Good to go."

"Really?"

"Yup, you know … to help me sleep."

"It sounded like you slept pretty good to me."

"Well, I'm on vacation, and since I don't partake in these types of activities on the daily, I'm inclined to indulge, no?"

"I'm not saying anything. I'm glad about it."

I shouldered the duffel bag like a backpack. The tools shuffled, clinking metal that lured Three Bands' attention, who was now sipping his second beer. "Let's go." I led us through the cabin door and back onto the sandy bank.

Robert Dean followed and brushed beside me. "In a hurry?"

"Aren't you?"

Three Bands exited the cabin and leapt to the beach.

This time, I didn't wait for his spear to find my back. I led the way.

*****

I trudged along the best I could, and layered in dried sweat, my skin itched, and my body began to emit a deep funk. We kept on until we reached the skiff, moored at the far end from the houseboat—where the southeastern tip met the mangroves. Along the way, nothing seemed out of the ordinary. People moved about the camp, strolling the trails without display, yet with purpose. Women and younger children followed in small factions, while the older ones promenaded in their own, private groups, as any teenagers might. Their instincts, it seemed, were much like ours, though they lived far removed from ordinary society.

We finally reached the bank of the canal, where my skiff appeared to have been left alone, sitting still in water two feet deep, wedged up against a cluster of mangroves. Its engine was tilted halfway out of the water, exposing a bit of the sun-reflective stainless propeller. The white deck blinded me as I stepped closer. In the console holders, my rods stood still and upright, and the baitwell remained full of stagnant, tea-colored water, and stunk of dead bait.

Tiku must have been repairing the illegal net, the same one we hit strung across the canal, and somehow matched it to my skiff. Not a hard find since the mesh had obviously been sliced using a sharp, fast-moving object.

It took me a moment to find balance on the bow of my skiff, undulating a small wave that blended into a soft ripple, which an easy morning breeze had already provided.

Robert Dean joined me, sending the bow down. He whispered: "We should clear this thing out and leave these sons-of-bitches behind!"

"Can't. Houseboat."

"Shamus, I'd say leave it. I'll buy yah a new one, better one."

"Oooh no, I've spent a lot of time and *plenty* of *your* money fixing her up—no way. If, and I say *if* we leave, we're taking both vessels with us. Earlier you said you'd like to stay and *learn* something?"

He faced Three Bands and Tiku, who balanced on an extending bushel of mangrove. "Well, what about the plan then?" His spoke in cautious strokes, as if our captures understood. "You know, fix this prop and get the hell out of here? Your words, remember…?"

"I did remember saying that, and I plan on executing it, but you know, it might take coordination on our part. There are two—" I held up two fingers like a peace sign. "…vessels to sneak out of here."

"Okay," he said, lowering to one knee and adjusting his tone. "Then let's get to thinkin' of a plan."

I laid the duffel bag on the deck, opened it, and dipped my body into the water, and even though the temperature was that of bathwater, its coolness was immediate.

Flip-flops weren't ideal for wading, and after the first step, the marl began to suction down my foot, pulling my leg deep into the earth. I jerked up my knee, then foot, stretching out the flip-flop toe strap close to the breaking point. Thinking how miserable life would be to walk around the shell-laden village lacking the proper foot protection, I reached down and methodically un-wedged the sole.

Across the propeller, I glanced at the mangrove bank. On the cusp of a mangrove thicket, our eager onlookers were perched, studying my every move. If Three bands and the kid progressed any deeper, they'd blend right in.

I shook my head back into focus, and now with the lower-unit and half the propeller raised from the water, I set my eyes on task, refreshing my sleep-deprived mind on the current situational details. Obviously, the netting had tangled the propeller well, so removing it was the only option.

"Hand me the socket?" I said to Robert Dean.

He began to rummage through the bag. While he was busy, Tiku eyeballed my casting rod. He whispered something to Three Bands like a shy kid afraid to approach an adult.

I called out, "Go right ahead." Then added a nod.

Three Bands' eyes slanted, gave the okay, and the youngster leaped onto the bow.

Robert Dean became interested, too. "What's he doin' now?"

"He's interested in the rods," I said. "Might as well let him check it out. I mean, what's the harm at this point, right?"

"True."

I grinned. "Plus, aren't you the least bit curious how he might react?"

"Not at all," Robert Dean replied quickly, and handed me the socket wrench.

I took it and applied it to the castle nut. "This isn't the right size, man. Give me the twenty-five millimeter."

Robert Dean opened the bag and shuffled. "It ain't in here, Shamus." He looked to make sure.

"What? It has to be in there. I just used it the other—" That's when it hit me. I'd used it the other day to take off this same propeller after Gina from Wisconsin decided to play captain. "Oh, crap."

Robert Dean saw my expression change. "What?"

"Um…"

"You forgot it, didn't you? You forgot the stinkin' right size? Oh, Shamus…"

"Yep," I said, scratching my head. "But hang on a second. I might be able to use the Channel Locks."

Robert Dean shuffled again through the bag.

I said, "Let me guess, not there?"

"Correct-o."

I shook my head. "I know there's a pair of needle-nose pliers in there, so hand me those, okay?"

He reached in like it was a candy-filled grab-bag—then stretched out his hand clenching the needle-nose instead. "These work?"

"Will have to," I replied.

Robert Dean shook his head. "Shamus, that's a castle nut, and I'm not sure those needles are goin' do it now, but you go ahead and try."

"Condescending, aren't we?" I mumbled.

"What?"

"Nothing. Let me remove the cotter pin first and see. I didn't tighten the nut very well. These threads are reversed … keeps them tight against the prop's force."

My friend turned, watched Tiku examining the rod.

The child's eyes tried to make sense of the corked-handle grip, and then the reel. He squinted to protect his eyes as he plucked at the braided line like a banjo string.

I said to Robert Dean, "Go ahead, show him a thing or two. I dare you."

"I think he'll figure it out by his own self."

"Considering all the events that have transpired in front of us in the last twenty-four hours, please tell me what on earth you witnessed that could *possibly* lead you to say anything like that with a straight face?"

Robert Dean rolled off one knee and stepped to Tiku at the center console and snatched the rod from the kid's hands. First words to the boy were, "You ain't even holdin' it right. Here, like this." He demonstrated how to hold the rod one handedly, down to finger placement—tone abrasive.

Even though Kitu didn't appear to be his son, Three Bands had instinctual parental protection blooming in the eyes. I didn't think he cared much for Robert Dean. With the current language barrier, tenor went a long way, and my friend's brute force personality was obviously fueling his cautionary approach.

Robert Dean was now occupied, so I inspected the four-blade and pondered, knew the castle nut wasn't the problem. I then used the pliers and threaded the needle-nose tip through the cotter pinhole and yanked. It slid out halfway. I placed the pin between my lips like a toothpick, and using the needle-nose pliers again, loosened the castle nut and placed both pin and nut on the corner of the portside stern hatch.

I glanced up at Robert Dean as he whipped out the lure, shooting it into the air, pulling off yards of braid. Both Tiku and Three Bands gazed, locked in amazement, tracking the projectile as is arced into the sky.

After a splash landing, my friend began reeling in the lure using a walk-the-dog-technique. "See? Are you watching? It's that easy. All yah gotta do is let the line go at juuust the right time." After a few casts, he handed off the fishing rod. "Now you," he said.

The reel's handle immediately befuddled the child. He tried to spin it backwards at first, where the anti-reverse feature activated. "Not like that. C'mon now," Robert Dean said and removed his handkerchief from his blue jean overall's pocket, and in frustration, wiped his forehead. I let out a light chuckle.

My friend critiqued Tiku's gritty attempts at casting a few more times before stepping back to the stern. He leaned over the poling platform. "You done yet?"

"Almost," I answered.

He grinned slightly. "I've never heard of anyone taking so long just to remove a prop before."

"If I had the right tools, I'd be more inclined to meet your busy schedule."

"Who forgot what?" he challenged.

"Aren't you enjoying yourself?"

"Actually, I was, thank yah very much."

"Is he getting it? Understanding the process of a cast? Better finish up with him, I'm almost done here."

Robert Dean leaned off the platform and returned to one knee. "He can finish himself. I mean, hard to believe these dirt lovers haven't even seen no fishin' poles before."

I paused at my friend's comment. "It's hard to believe? What's harder to believe is that this weird society was able to slip by the real world for as long as they have. It's weird, this part of the Cutoff had always been untapped, but never *this* untapped. It appears they've lived here a long time—maybe tens of years—maybe longer…" I glanced up from the prop.

I was talking to myself. Robert Dean was watching his back, not paying attention to me.

Three Bands was balancing, surveilling from a mangrove small limb. I could tell he wanted to try the new fish device but was reluctant to ask.

Robert Dean leaned in, saw me untangling the fibrous netting from the propeller shaft. "You got a plan yet … for gettin' the heck outta here? I could use a beer right about now."

I shrugged. "Hand me the prop."

He did.

I said, "For one, I think we need to move the skiff next to the houseboat. That'll give us an easier way of leaving … at the same time … with both vessels."

"I hear yah. Sneak out at the same time, good idea."

I corrected him. "Not sure *at* the same time is what I mean."

He suggested, "What I was thinkin' is that we just get this prop un-fouled and go, *but…*"

"What?" I cut in, then realized I'd been set up. A father's instinct sparked up when he taught the child how to use the rod.

"I'm just playin' with you." He glanced again at Tiku. "I say we just go ahead and take the skiff up to the bank, park her right next to the houseboat, and get us some *real* breakfast. Well, lunch now…"

I'd been trying to avoid the thought of food after smelling the seafood plethora set out during the morning meal, so I wondered what Robert Dean meant by "real lunch."

"Okay, so this is the plan," I said, then slid the bright, sun-reflecting stainless-steel propeller onto the shaft. "Once I get this thing tight and good to go, I'll get a quick feel for things and start the engine. Test the waters."

Robert Dean grinned, understanding my ploy. "Test the waters, huh…?"

"Yeah."

His eyes found Three bands on the limb. "I'm okay with that…" he added.

I finished lining up the castle nut, which I hand-tightened. Next, I lined up the cotter pin and slid it through the hole in the shaft. Once satisfied, and inching my fingers toward the trim located on the engine's left side, I said, "Pssssst" to Robert Dean, then winked toward the bow.

"What?" he asked.

"Little warmup." I pressed the trim button.

A high-pitched whine hit Tiku's ears. His head jerked toward us like an owl spotting prey. He didn't seem afraid initially as he studied the engine lowering into the water. Tiku then faced us and shifted, slipping tentatively to the poling platform while his eyes locked on the engine. For his entertainment, I raised and lowered the engine a few more times while the little one observed, smiling and laughing—and his face, that of an early teen, curious and thirsty for knowledge.

"See … nothing to be scared of." Robert Dean's tone changed to a fatherly one. "I think he likes it."

"Likes it? I'm not sure he knows what the hell this thing is."

There was some fleeting enjoyment that I couldn't fight.

Robert Dean moved to the console. "Okay, that's enough with the warmup," he said and cranked the engine.

Tiku's reaction to the engine's soft reverberation through the skiff was anything but calm—his body tense, eyes alert. In a sudden burst, he leapt from the bow into the mangrove where Three Bands clung, nearly knocking them both into the water.

Robert Dean turned to me. "I guess he wasn't ready for that one."

"Unbelievable. I thought you two were hitting it off—then you go and do that?"

"Oh, I'm just messin' with him. He'll be fine." Robert Dean believed it—then added, "Even your buddy cracked a smile."

Truth. Three Bands smile was cheap, a half-bent crack, no eye involvement, which said plenty of his relationship with Robert Dean.

Since the engine was running, and the idea of piloting the skiff toward the northern village's rim fresh, now seemed like as good a time as any, and a risk worth taking.

I motioned for Robert Dean to remove the shallow water anchor—a long PVC pipe dug into the muck.

Three Bands pointed his spear toward my friend, waved Robert Dean to de-board the vessel.

"Ummm…" my friend said.

I whispered, "I think he wants you to get off."

"Yah *think*…?"

At portside, using one leg, I rolled myself into the boat and sat to the side, shaking the mud from my flops like a kid sitting poolside thrashing his feet.

Robert Dean's heavy movement rocked the boat—resisting. "Now, you just hang on a minute. We're *juuust* goin' move it. That's all, bud."

Three Bands face was unresponsive.

"I don't think he cares. He's smart. Doesn't want us taking off for some reason, and he's using you as leverage."

His chest rose. "Nobody uses Robert Dean as leverage—"

"Just stay," I told him.

"Stay?"

"Yes, it's no big deal. I'll meet you by the houseboat in a little bit."

Robert Dean settled, tracked Three Bands, then sucked in his cheek, trying to get a read on the man. After seconds of stalemate, he said, "How do I know he ain't gonna fingerprint me again … and allow that crazy, black-masked bastard to lay me out again … on that cold stone table? Huh?"

"Good point. Well…" I lowered to my voice to a whisper. "If you just quit being so abrasive and let the *gentle* Robert Dean do the talking, then you should be fine."

"Gentle Robert Dean? Ha!" He turned back toward Three Bands. "Fine, whatever. I'll stay, and you go take your skiff up." He paused—added, "But, Shamus, if you leave me, *so help me* God."

A large ripple rolled into the creek when Three Bands' massive size leapt onto the bow of the skiff, landing in a surfer's stance. He pointed Robert Dean off the boat, to the mangroves next to Tiku, but before exiting, Robert Dean snatched the fishing rod.

I was unsure whether Three Bands knew of our plans to sneak the skiff to the houseboat. Maybe he wanted to take the skiff for a test ride? His intentions were difficult to read. It seemed more as if he'd been instructed to, more or less, "handle us." Let us wander and observe, but not in a way that gave us the ability to escape—that had been made clear. Letting Robert Dean leave with Tiku was the most confusing element of all.

I geared the engine in reverse. Robert Dean nosed the bow away from the mangroves using his boot. I gave him one final smile.

"Have fun with *your* new buddy," he said.

I smiled back. "You too."

Chapter Twelve

I nosed the skiff into the open Cutoff, making berth at idle speed while my new buddy sat on the cushion ahead of the console, his size making it difficult to navigate. As I began to turn, heading down the starboard finger creek back to the houseboat, he waved me out toward the open Cutoff.

Once I had a good line-of-sight into the open water, I tapped the throttle and sped up, just a tick. Three Bands gripped the handrail as he detected it could get bumpy. I felt confident and slammed the throttle, sending the skiff on a smooth plane. I was driving aimlessly. Three Bands' long hair flapped in chaos, sending a homemade hair tie flying into the wash of our wake. He clenched the straying strands, clumped them as one, twisted it tight, and let it go.

While reaching our top speed of thirty knots, the midday sun glistened off the water's mirrored surface. Three Bands adjusted fine to the speed—tight-gripped to the handrail.

I brought us deeper into the mangroves toward the northern portion of the Cutoff where he waved. As we closed in on a charter spot I knew well, Three Bands arms flailed and pointed toward a side creek.

I idled the skiff toward the small cut, into a place I'd fished many times, where half submerged clump of oysters clamped to the red roots of mangroves, exposing sharp shelled tips.

Off our flank, a large squawking gray heron, standing in knee-deep water, decided to take flight. I usually paid no attention to a squawking bird, but Three Bands studied it, the direction it flew, as though making mental notes.

Once we reached the heart of the creek, he revealed his reason for his zeal. From one end of the creek to the other, they'd strewn across the identical palm fiber mesh net we'd sliced to pieces earlier. Two spikes anchored on each side held it in place brilliantly, like an underwater volleyball net. Impressively, the net had been placed in areas where the water had the most prolific flow. It was an illegal gillnet.

For safety and obvious reasons, I shut the engine off and drifted toward the portside anchor pole of the net.

Three Bands used his lanky arms to reach for the top of the pole. He jerked it from the muck, laid the muddy pole on the front deck, and began pulling the headrope. I marveled at the strength of the mesh, where groupings of mollusk shell held the footrope anchored.

As he pulled in the rope, as if expected, flickering black-spotted tails rose to the surface.

He reached down and snatched one of the thrashing tails, then flipped the first fish onto the deck. Using one hand, he pinned the fish and punched it using the other. After two massive blows, he'd rendered the fish unresponsive.

I glanced around for witnesses. "What are you doing?" I muttered to myself. "You'll get me arrested."

Although an illegal method, and judging from the number of villagers to feed, I had to trust that he'd never been caught. He did this to ten other fish, ranging from giant snook to the smallest sugar trout.

Once satisfied, as though it were a tailgate, he left the skiff, leaping into the water. He began rolling the net up like a large blueprint, wading through the darkest corridor of the creek, deep to his waist, pinning the opposite end to a mangrove branch—un-setting the net. If he was doing what I thought, then it was a smart move. With the tide being low, most fish were vacant from the creeks. When the tide returned in a few hours, the fishes would repopulate. After which, the net would be reset for an outgoing tide.

He loaded back in the skiff, and I puttered from the creek, then inched us charily above idle speed. At our gaining speed, Three Bands swiped his hand through the air, wanted me off plane.

As I placed the boat in neutral, he removed a tiny mollusk shell from a small pouch on the side of his loincloth.

Before slicing open the belly of the first fish, he slid the shell's sharpest edge across his tongue as if warming it up. He then deliberately selected the largest snook, cradled it in his arms, and proceeded to saw using the mollusk knife, bursting open the snook's belly.

I remembered the spare bait knife stowed in the front hatch. I declined the thought. So far, these dwellers didn't seem to need any help from me.

One by one, he gutted each fish the same. Under the scales and along the spine, his precision was admirable and eloquent as he sliced through the flesh. He piled the guts onto the bow, and if he found roe, he ate it onsite. There were many studies that found fish eggs to contain massive amounts of Vitamin D and Omega-3 fatty acids—things the body requires to stay healthy—a bonus find for a growing hunter. He finished nearly ten fish and pointed me to return to the village.

*****

We glided onto the mangrove bank to a crowd loitering near the houseboat. I beached the skiff next to it and immediately heard a voice: "You made it!"

Robert Dean stuck his head from the port-side cabin door and smiled.

"What's he up to…?" I mumbled to myself.

Three Bands leaped off the bow, and using the bow mooring rope, pulled the skiff up onto the beach like beaching any one of the dugout canoes.

I tilted the engine up, exposing the shiny propeller while noticing Three Bands summoning his minions to, I assume, take care of the day's knockouts.

After deboarding, I slipped to the port-side pontoon, realized Robert Dean wasn't alone in the cabin of the houseboat. I climbed up and entered the cabin to find three topless women standing along the doorway leading into the head, inspecting the compacted facility.

I found Robert Dean showing Tiku my tackle box. Using the galley table, he'd spread out samples of hooks, top-water lures, and soft plastics. He held my twenty-pound fluorocarbon leader and was cinching it tight through the eye of a hook while Tiku studied like an erudite student.

Robert Dean began connecting the two ends. "Now, see? This knot is called a double-uni." He said it like ooooni. "What this does is it ties yer leader to yer braid, see?" He held up the two ends so the youngster could see.

I stepped into his space and grinned. "Nice. Getting along pretty well, yes?"

"Oh, I'm just givin' him a few pointers is all, no big deal." The significance of my friend's willingness to help after these men had nearly shattered his shins to bits, was quite the flight. I let him be.

At the head sliding door, the women were peering into the bathroom and down at the toilet, giggling with interest. They were shoeless and topless but dressed in identical moss skirts. From head to toe their bodies were equally tanned and had hair like yarn, tied up above round, happy faces.

I tried not to stare at their half-naked bodies, focusing instead on whatever held their interest, and squeezed past them into the bathroom. I unzipped and began to urinate. After I finished, I sat, simulating it also had another usage.

Giggles became louder as they marveled at the toilet.

I then wedged through the tight doorway, and before I was completely out, they shimmied in, rubbing bare chests against mine. Holding my hands up, I let all three women pass, shut the door, and let them be.

"They been at the door for well over an hour," Robert Dean said.

"Why didn't you show them how to … you know … go?"

"Ahh, too busy with junior here. Very smart this one." He handed the fishing line to the eager-awaiting kid. "Okay, you try." He then stepped over to me, jerked a thumb at the bathroom door. "Hope you showed 'em how to flush."

I began a thin, half-hearted smile, and said in regret, "I did *not*. That's what you're for."

"I'm not cleaning that up. Nooo way, Shamus. Not with their fishy diet … oooooh-no."

"Don't worry, I'll figure it out." I nodded to the skiff. "Should have seen the pigs we pulled from the creek toward the back of the Cutoff—monsters, biggest snook I've ever seen."

"Oh, yeah? Did you and Crazy Horse fish … with the rods?"

I found his eyes. "More gillnets across the canal."

"Wow," Robert Dean peeked through the cabin window towards the beach. "No shame in their game. I guess yah gotta do what yah gotta do. Far be it from me to say anything."

"Yeah, I watched him shake and untangle snook after snook into the boat, just waiting for FWC to appear around the corner."

Robert Dean replied, "I'm not sure these people are caught often."

"That's what I'm thinking too…"

My friend moseyed back next to Tiku.

I mulled deep over my friend's level of commitment, whether it had drifted or not, so I asked, "Tonight we make our move, okay?"

"You betcha," he said, and continued to instruct the kid.

After twenty minutes, the door to the head flew open.

Robert Dean said, "Told you."

I pointed to the door. "That's *your* department."

Puffing out cheeks, the women scurried from the houseboat, leaped into the water, and bathed in the creek. I watched through the cabin window as they waded to the bank, where Three Bands was still separating the fish as the women fish-fillet-ers, waited, clenching, sharpening their stone knives.

The bathroom smell reached my nose. "You should get on that," I told him. "If someone lights a match, we'll blow."

My friend left the table and flushed the toilet. "I don't even smell it anymore," he replied, sniffing in a deep breath. "So, what did you have in mind tonight … escape-wise?"

"I think we've somewhat gained their trust, just enough to let us wander a bit. I mean, we're back on the houseboat so…"

He suggested, "Let's wait until dark."

"Agreed."

"What if they're guardin' the boat again?"

I removed my white visor and ran a hand through my shaggy brown hair, tried to conjure up an appropriate answer, settled on, "I'm not sure."

"I say we take them out," he said. "The guards."

"Take them out? I hope you don't mean *kill.*"

"Oh, c'mon Shamus, I'm just saying we knock 'em out or something." He breathed, opened his eyes wide. "Incapaci-TATE."

"Didn't we try that already? Remember? It didn't go so well…"

"That's good for us, yah see?" He winked. "They'll never suspect us to try it again…"

I weighed his suggestion. "Hmm, might work." Then I pointed my finger. "But *no* killing, got it?"

"What makes you think I'm capable of killin' a man?"

"I'm not sure, but who knows what goes on up there in those lawless mountains of yours."

He grinned. "You don't worry about that. We take gooood care of *ourselves.*"

I shook my head. "I bet you do."

Robert Dean snapped his tone back to serious. "Now, I say we keep playing this little game they got going on here for a little while longer. Then 'round midnight, we sneak back here and *poof,* we're gone."

I nodded. "I think that's simple and will work."

"So, it's a plan then? We stick around for now, lay low, maybe eat, and later tonight, we break free?"

"Sounds good to me," I said.

Then, a slight list of the houseboat. Stomps made their way along the gunwale. Through the cabin door swooped Three Bands with the spear.

Robert Dean stiffened straight as though Three Bands was a drill sergeant. "Why is he always carryin' that thing?" he said from the corner of his mouth.

"Seems he only carries it when you're around…"

"Funny."

"It's true."

Tiku sat at attention alongside us.

Three Bands said something that sounded like, *"Carjama geeto muna."* Whatever it was, Tiku understood, and line-tying time was now over. He raced out, and before I knew it, was high-tailing it down the short, sandy bank, through the trail, and down the wall of shells.

Three Bands looked at me, then Robert Dean. His eyes locked on my friend, and he motioned the spear for us both to exit.

Once on the beach, he shuffled us toward the fish tables. Spread across a small section of remaining beach lay their chewed up woven mesh fish net—identical to the one Three Bands and I pulled the fish from. Except this one was torn to pieces.

Robert Dean said, "Looks like more of the net we ran over."

"Sure is," I replied, as I examined my friend's clothes down to his boots.

His blue jean suspenders had been dyed brown from the dirt and saltwater mixture. His white T-shirt had moistened to a dark brown blend of sweat and dirt. One thing that I wished I had that Robert Dean had was his boots. My friend wore boots no matter what the event was—a characteristic of a life lived in the mountains. While my feet were sliced and diced from all the scattered shell bits, Robert Dean's remained dry and protected.

Three Bands said, "Caaat."

I looked at Robert Dean.

Three Bands said again, "Caaat."

"I think he's saying *cut*," I side-lipped to my friend.

"Now, how is he all of a sudden goin' start speakin' English?"

"I'm not sure … it sounded like he said *cut*."

"Like … the line is cut?"

"Exactly."

He said side-lipped, "Thought we already banged that chicken…"

I grinned, then pulled back.

Robert Dean suddenly stepped forward. "Now, you don't worry about that. We'll fix it, nooo problem." He raised his hand and snatched the net. "Nothing to fancy getting upset about, just more torn net, no need yah to worry." He spread the net out like gingerbread men cut from paper.

"How are we going to fix that?" I said. "It probably took them a month to make it."

Three Bands stood, spear dug in the ground, holding his leaning weight.

My friend moved in closer. "I'm just sayin' that so these dirt dwellers don't do anything that would keep us from our plan, see?"

I replied, "I understand, but it appears that with these people? Actions speak louder than words."

"We already removed their net from our flippin' prop. What more do they want?" Robert Dean balled up the net like a dirty paper towel and tossed it onto the picnic table, as if making a fade-away jumper to a trashcan. He held up his finger and said, "Be right back," and made for the houseboat.

Three Bands swung the spear, aimed it again, but my friend kept on walking.

He began shuffling around in the houseboat, and after a short while emerged carrying the same fishing pole that he had used to teach Tiku.

"Here, take this."

He handed Three Bands the rod, who didn't part from a rigid posture.

"Okay, okay. I'll just leave it here." Robert Dean leaned the rod against the table. He stepped back to me wiping his hands, and said, "Problem solved."

I frowned. "You know that rod cost me over three-hundred dollars—"

"I'll get you a new one," he said from the corner of his mouth.

Robert Dean's offering really grinded my gears, but I had to admit, it was good thinking—and quick.

Three Bands appeared to be in a state of limbo on the offering. He wielded the spear in attack mode and shifted sight between the fishing rod, and us.

"I'm not sure that'll do it," I said from the corner of *my* mouth.

"Why not? That rod is plenty more valuable than his ol' hippie net."

"Did you see how many people are living here? These people need to buy in bulk, if you know what I mean."

"Well, let's just wait a flappin' minute ... see what he does first."

We both noticed Three Bands' mind calculating. While we waited, the group of women who had used the head on the houseboat skipped along the sand bank and off down the wall of shells. They vanished behind palm tree shadows.

Robert Dean leaned sideways. "Be right back." In the houseboat, he shuffled things again and materialized carrying something in his hand. He moved in, dodged the spear's stone tip, offered Three Bands a beer, said, "Beeeer. Go ahead now—take it."

Three Band's expression changed, and he flipped down the spear, spiked it into the sand. He accepted the beer, and after sliding a long fingernail under the tab, popped the carbonation.

Robert Dean helped as he sipped. "There yah go … easy now." He raised his chin, guiding the liquid.

I grinned, shook my head, and whispered, "Unbelievable."

Three Band's easy sipping expanding into a guzzle.

"That was genius," I said.

"I think there's enough to keep him *ocupado* for a good while."

I said, "What's *my* name, Skip?"

Robert Dean bolted again for the houseboat and returned gripping two beers in each hand. He cracked one open, handed it to me, then cracked one for himself.

We both gulped healthy mouthfuls, but had eyes on Three Bands shaking the can, listening for liquid.

"He's out," I said.

Robert Dean moved forward, and using a single hand, cracked the top of the can using his index finger, a simultaneous handoff to Three Bands.

He accepted the second beer, then my friend gestured with his beer against mine for cheers. I cheered his can, and we reached for Three Bands. He hesitated.

"Cheers," Robert Dean said, repeating cheers to me, and right after, back at the tall, tan man. This time Three Bands arm extended, and suspiciously, returned the strange ritualistic levity.

We drank.

*****

I was now confident enough to relax, so we sat at the empty food table next to the fish table. Three Bands stomped off to give instructions to his clan of soldiers, who stood a stone's throw away.

I said, "That wasn't so bad."

My exhausted friend swiped out a handkerchief, wiped his forehead, "Seriously, I'll get yah another rod."

"I know you will."

As we sat at the homemade, and surprisingly durable table, food preparation began at the adjacent tables.

A breeze swept down the canal and across the tables. Light was sufficient inside the camp, slicing through the crispy palm fronds that dangled dead under their crowns. It seemed the tables may have been constructed to rest in direct sunlight at certain times of the day.

Women cleaned the fish like robots, slicing the meat into chunks, then those chunks into smaller portions. Then laying them out in neat rows. They loaded the clean-cut fish heads into a large pot sitting above a smoldering fire. When the wind was true, I felt its heat on my face.

"Fish soup," Robert Dean said.

What remained of the carcass, the women loaded into the beached canoes.

He added, "I bet they're taking the rest of the fish out to the nets. Maybe draw in more fish or crab."

Every so often, a woman would break her stoic expression and glance our way. She was curious about our attendance. She was also young—maybe twenty years old, still had the skinny of youth. She produced a slender, white-toothed smile.

"I think she likes you," I said to Robert Dean.

"Me? Nah, she's looking at you, Shamus."

She returned to her duty of cleaning the fish.

Robert Dean inspected Three Bands while he stood erect, instructional, speaking an unknown language to the five, spear-wielding, listening men while expressing his thoughts using hand motions. He said, "I wonder what he's telling them."

"Me too."

"I'm not sure, but what I'm wonderin' is, if he leaves us here, we could haul out right this minute."

"I thought you wanted to stay for a bit longer?"

"I'm just sayin' that if he goes off and leaves us here, we could bolt."

My friend was correct. We'd placed the vessels in perfect proximity to each other—the skiff's propeller un-fouled and ready to go. If the three-banded-man did leave us at our leisure, while sitting on this table right next to our escape boats, sneaking out, preferably unnoticed, was plausible.

I said, "You know, we might be able to make it … I mean if he leaves."

Robert Dean kept his sights on Three Bands, surveying his movements, actions, mannerisms.

Then Tiku shot through an unmarked trail, hit the short bank running hard, tracked up to Three Bands, and spoke furiously. Like a quarterback in a huddle, Three Bands said one more thing to the men before they broke and ran toward us.

"Here we go again," Robert Dean said.

The men jogged in our direction; spears leveled in attack position.

"What now?" Robert Dean said again.

"I have no clue."

The men jogged past us as though we didn't exist, boarded the canoes, and shoved off—two in one and three in the other. Silent paddles sank into the water, and before we could figure out what was happening, the men pressed the canoe forward, making way, disappearing around a mangrove point.

"That was weird," Robert Dean said. "Probably goin' out to fish."

We focused back on the houseboat. Three Bands now stood rigid next to us—again with spear.

"Greaaat," my friend said.

Three Bands waved the spear in the direction of the wall of shells. Insinuated: "You know the drill."

We didn't resist.

"I don't get this guy," my friend said, mid-breath, in mid-step along the shell-laden path.

"Yeah, I'm not sure anymore either."

"I mean, one minute we're all drinkin' a beer and what-have-you … having a good ol' time, and then he brings out the stinkin' spear again. I mean, what's his deal?"

"I hear you," I said. "I'm not sure either, but it seems to be very important for him to maintain a warrior bravado."

"Well, I think at this point he could lose the spear … is all I'm sayin'."

I kept quiet, stomped along the path, marveling at all the shells in ornate alignment—row after row. Some still containing silver-blue reflective innards. We'd walked a decent distance so far. The path we used earlier was approaching fast, and once we arrived at its trailhead, I rested. Oddly, the stone tip from Three Bands' spear no longer touched the small of my back. I pointed, gesturing toward the right-handed trail. Three Bands nodded yes, and I went through.

We kept on, and I could only assume he was leading us back to our primitive motel accommodations. We again passed the small dwelling of the sweeping woman, but she was no longer in sight. As we breezed past the hut, people gathered ahead, lingering at the entrance to what was now known as the burial grounds.

The villagers, a group of twenty, were patiently awaiting permission to enter. Three Bands had made our arrival fully noticeable and obvious while he fastened us to the end of the line.

Chapter Thirteen

As we neared the entrance to the burial ground, it became clear we would need permission to enter. "Now we got to go to a funeral?" my friend said.

"Apparently," I replied. "It seems we're getting the *whole* experience."

We remained in line, and the villagers who'd been denied entry began to contemplate us. They didn't stare out of frustration or indifference but showed us expressions of sympathy and concern.

Inside, something powerful, maybe spiritual was taking place, and while approaching the man who guarded the entrance, the mood changed as though my conscious mind had been injected with leaden vibes of glum. I chose not to fight it.

Three Bands let go and eased back from the group. The others followed, but they were young and restless, lingering like tarpon nosing a dock light, not sure whether to strike or drift away. Robert Dean's silence signified that the gloomy vibe had also infected him.

A man at the head of the line held a pencil-sized twig from a wild oak; a smoking streamer spiraled up from its tip—similar to incense. He waved the smoke ring counterclockwise, circling the proceeding villagers' round, somber faces. After each person, he blew the ember tip red hot, producing the proper amount of thick smoke to complete one full rotation.

After a few minutes in line, we reached the entrance to the burial ground. Once there, the short man, whose head was bald and weighed down by a shell-filled necklace, paused in skepticism, then faced Robert Dean and me. He didn't wear the themed loincloth as the other men—but wore the common Spanish moss skirt of the women. With hair so white, his face looked like a winter wonderland. He had a choice to make. After he glanced at Three Bands, his expression changed from confusion to approval and started a smoke ring around my head. I remained still as a dead gator, allowing the smoke ring to engulf my face. I was granted full access.

Robert Dean waited in line; he also needed permission to enter. Three Bands signaled using his chin.

My friend held back a laugh as the smoke consumed his face. But he remained composed long enough to arrive by my side.

Inside, the space stretched as wide as a basketball court, yet felt hollow, nearly vacant. No more than a dozen had been admitted—men, women, and children gathered together, drawn toward a single, intentional corner of the clearing. Three Bands spoke to the guard at the entrance.

Robert Dean whispered, "They're goin' make us watch a fricken burial, I know it."

"I think you're right, and I bet those people…" I nodded toward the group of villagers "…over there are family and friends of the deceased."

Robert Dean shook his head. "All I want to do is get some fricken food … we've all been to funerals before. I mean, is this even necessary?"

I understood my friend's frustrations, but death was a serious event, and the unforeseen community wanted to share it with us.

While Robert Dean rambled on about his hunger, the group huddled above someone, like an injured athlete on a field of play.

Robert Dean also noticed. "Looks like it's about to start."

Over toward the entrance, Three Bands spoke ardently to the man who spiraled our faces in smoke.

Robert Dean's head faced down, and using his boots, kicked a small hole in the shell ground. A sharp shell chunk landed on my bare toes. "Dude, chill out."

"I just want food."

Robert Dean swiped his boot once more.

Three Bands' conversation ended, and he stomped our way.

"Here he comes now," my friend whispered.

Neither one of us gave him respect or straightened up or acted interested as he arrived. He held the spear vertically toward the group and signaled for us to follow. We did, but not before Robert Dean let our irritation be known using a sigh.

We reached the huddled group after what seemed like a split second. The group began to separate for us like a doctor's incision, exposing the person for whom the gathering was defined.

What caught my eye first was that this person, while not at all dead, lay flat, head propped upon a pillow, similar to what they gave Robert Dean and me. He was old, frail, and his soft skin was as though, if touched, might crack like wet paper. He had no facial hair, but the same round face, and instead of tan, he was ghostly, pale gray, like a fine layer of dust. A ponytail wrapped a wrinkled neck and ended on his chest while a furry deer hide covered him from chest to toes. His hands rested along his sides, fingers full of gold rings. His right hand was curled in atrophy; the left side of his face drooped, sagging open his eye, revealing the red orbit underneath. It was clear that his time was coming to an end.

We waited ten minutes for something to happen. The dying man winced in pain and was increasingly blanched after every breath. Ambient whispers from the villagers confirmed that their funereal sadness was real, but they shed no tears. Next to him, a man finished digging a shallow grave, no more than a foot deep.

As my attention lay on the dying man, soft whispers of the unknown tongue came to an abrupt stop, and their focus turned toward the entrance.

Robert Dean said, "Here we go again."

Chief entered the clearing unannounced, passing under the green palm frond altar. He strode, stepped, and paused, stepped and paused, as though pacing down the aisle at a wedding.

His wife walked the same, a couple people-lengths behind him, and instead of a Spanish moss skirt, a black-netted skirt covered her waist down to her knees. And dangling above, teabag-sized, black-plated circular earrings stretched through her large, dilated lobes. She wore the same eagle headband and carried a clear stein in her hand.

As they made their way toward us, Chief's eye makeup had been reapplied, giving it a rich, bloody boldness. He had no intimidating expression, and once he was halfway close, a chant began.

"*Benga benga oonna … benga benga oonna.*"

After chanting it twice, the others echoed him. By the halfway point, he was repeating the chant with every step. The dying man, mustering all his remaining breath, he too said the chant.

Robert Dean elbowed me. "I hope they ain't to pile all those shells on top of this guy … alive."

"Hard to say…"

My friend was right. Next to the sick man, they'd piled waist high various types of shells that I know to be everything from mollusks to oysters.

Chief shuffled himself closer and closer. A satchel strap crossed his chest, its main bulk rested behind him.

Between chants, under their feet, shells crunched, inserting a layer of miasmic eeriness, that frankly gave me the goosebumps. Once Chief reached the group, he motioned us back to Three Bands' side. He used his hands, not the spear.

When the dying man saw Chief, his head suddenly jerked toward him, then he tried to speak in a short, hushed moan. Chief knelt next to him and held his pale, gaunt hand.

With a firm hold on the incense stick, the white-bearded man knelt too, but on the opposite side, and with both men beside the dying man, his feet began to fidget. His weak hand gradually lifted away from the Chief's hand. He requested something. Chief held his hand again, patted it, lowered it back to his chest, reached to the satchel, and removed the contents.

I was stunned by what the chief held in his tight grasp. The dying man's eyes found the snake, and he reached for it again. The chief drew it back, but the sick man strained toward it, summoning all he had to touch it—only for the chief to jerk it away once more.

I asked Robert Dean, "What is going on here?" I knew the answer.

"He's goin' have that snake bite him, I *know* it."

"You might be right," I said.

Robert Dean shook his head. "He better not do it. It ain't *right*."

"Ain't right?"

"Yes. Ain't ri-ght!"

I didn't answer and continued watching the ceremony.

Children in the clearing clung close to their mother's legs while craning little heads toward Chief in short bursts like a scared child watching a horror flick. While some were scared by the events, others seemed to be unphased by the ceremony. Either way, they were interested.

Chief began to chant. *"Benga benga oonna … Benga benga oonna."*

The dying man grew agitated, reached for Chief's arm again that held the moccasin. Chief's wife strode and knelt at the poor man's waist, settling next to the white-bearded man holding the incense stick. She gripped the sick man's atrophied hand, held it to her cheek, and while peering down into his eyes, said something too soft for our ears.

Three Bands remained attentive to us. I wandered to him, and he guided my eyes back to the ceremony like a teacher telling a student to face forward. I did.

The dying man paid close attention to the stein Chief's wife held.

"Is that water?" asked Robert Dean.

"I doubt it."

The dying man began kicking his feet like an irritated child.

This act of desperation caused Chief to wave the snake and chant. He leaned and signaled to his wife to raise the stein—she did.

"What's that wrapped around the snake's head?" asked Robert Dean.

Chief unwound the palm fiber strands from the snake's face, giving it space to commence a full mouth stretch, freeing needle-sharp fangs. Once the last rotation was completed, the snake's mouth strained open as it struggled to squirm its head free, but Chief held tight to its triangled head. He then presented it to the crowd, then leaned toward the stein. The snake squirmed again, wrapping its long, fat body around Chief's tan, slender arm. He maneuvered it into a milking position.

His wife's eyes fixated on the snake. From the handle, she held up the stein but wobbled it quite a bit. Once the snake came within inches, its jaws opened wide, exposing a white, wet mouth.

"Cottonmouth," said Robert Dean from the corner of his mouth.

Chief forced the snake's fangs onto the inner rim. A clear glass made it easy to see the syrupy venom dripping along the inside of the stein.

Once the snake had run dry of venom, Chief handed it off to a villager on standby who placed its head on a round, brown stone and chopped it off. A few of the people faced away while he tossed the snake's lower half to the ground, where it continued squiggling and squirming back and forth, trying to bite the air.

Chief began the chant again. *"Benga benga oonna … Benga benga oonna."* His voice was high-pitched but raspy, as though he used his diaphragm to push out his words.

The wife held the stein up to show the crowd, who reacted with heavy breaths and incisive claps.

Chief then reached behind himself, into the satchel. Out came a green, tightly wrapped palm frond. He ever-so-carefully unwrapped the envelope-sized frond, spreading apart the overlapping leaves. Before removing the final layer, he presented the frond to the crowd. After smashing it into his hands, he held the frond above the stein and wrung it dry—a hard squeeze, like procuring the last bit of juice from a lemon.

Robert Dean began to get antsy. "This ain't right, I'm tellin' yah."

"What ain't right?"

"This poor man … should be in a hospital."

"What hospital are you referring to, because I'm not seeing any?"

"You know what I'm sayin'." Robert Dean ended the conversation by folding his arms and chin-pointing in the dying man's direction.

Chief handed off the crumpled palm frond to the man on standby. He opened it, paid a few moments to the contents and, as if he'd done it a few times prior, handed it off to the next person—and so on. After a dozen people had handled it, it made its way to us. I opened it and saw what was left of a nest of spiders.

Robert Dean leaned in. "Oh-my-God … more stinkin' creepy crawlies."

What my friend and I saw were the remnants of countless spiders, their red hourglasses still visible on the small abdomens that had survived the crushing.

"Widows," I said.

"I ain't seen any kind of funeral like this before."

"Does anything about any of this seem normal? I mean, *look* around!"

"I'm just sayin…" Robert Dean shook his head. "Somethin' ain't right."

I didn't answer but focused on the crushed and smeared remnants of the black widow spiders. I made out three red abdomens pressed flat against the inside fold. Their small, thin legs tangled and overlapped. The insides, gooped and smeared together in a clump that resembled avocado dip. I folded it to its original form and handed it to the next awaiting person.

The wife rose, and out of a separate container, poured what reminded me of water into the stein and shook it vigorously like a bartender.

A sick as he was, the dying man attempted to sit up, but Chief prevented him using a gentle arm. He reached for the stein—the wife pulled it away.

A man then rushed into the burial area and slid on his knees into place next to the dying man.

Chief moved subtly, and he affably eased aside.

A spitting image of the dying man's—same nose, and round, dimpled chin, dying man and his companion embraced, and they spoke the un-intelligible language again.

Once the embrace had ended, the new man held his hand behind the dying man's head, to hold him into a sitting-up position. The dying man's companion received the stein from the grip of the chief's wife and handed it to the man of his blood.

It wobbled to his mouth, and he drank a resolute amount. His companion returned the stein to the wife, and afterwards, laid the dying man's head softly onto the pillow.

We waited for what I guess was … death.

Robert Dean leaned over again. "I don't think that snake venom and grounded up spiders'll kill yah."

"Really? That's what you've got to say about it?"

"Well…"

"You know, since he's so weak, the shock will probably stop his heart."

The man lay down, and after releasing a frightening cough, settled still, eyes waited open, peering straight up into the hazy overcast sky.

To wonder what it felt like to wait for someone's death had never crossed my mind, but now I had expert experience. The man wanted to die, and this community afforded him a choice, and he had chosen.

An exhalation was the next and final sign of life from him. He had expired and was silently lifted into the shell hole next to where he lay after the confirmation of death. His eyes remained open while the man who dug the grave began to bury the man in a conclusive covering of shell.

Immediately, the group dispersed. The new man stayed behind and proudly turned a hard ear up and faced the mound, as though listening to make sure no more of the sick man's breath would be heard. Three Bands led us clear from the cemetery and back on to the trail.

Robert Dean's voice rose to an agitated snarl. "They just killed that man. I saw it. We just witnessed a murder!"

"You've got to be kidding me," I replied, as we long-stepped away from the clearing.

"I think that that whole thin' back there could have been handled in a better way! There are hospitals in town, Shamus. Bury a guy in shell … yah don't see an issue here?"

"I don't think these people make it to town very often. Haven't you been paying attention?"

"I say we stick to the plan and head out later tonight … get out of this God-forsaken place."

I agreed in silence.

Chapter Fourteen

Back at our hut, a somber mood lingered after witnessing an assisted suicide. I sat on the threshold facing the trail and mumbled, "Can it really be called suicide?" The man was old and well-worn, had lived a full life and departed on his own terms. For Robert Dean to suggest that he witnessed a crime wasn't what I had expected from him. Dying on one's own terms is the richest kind of dignity. To deny this is a failure as to what it means to be human. Clearly the man had some sort of real sickness, and in pain.

I gazed at the shell path, to the fire pit, across to the cooking stone, where a slab of sizzling flesh rose smoke into the air. As it cooked, I thought about Sara and how she loves the light from a fire. "It's cozy," she'd say. Her thoughts inspired me to be good, and become noble, they were the *light* at the end of this dark road. I shook off the memory.

Robert Dean used a stick to poke the sizzling flesh. He sat on one of the two bench stumps. "Manatee," he said.

After a few minutes of cooking time my friend sliced open the meat, broke off a piece from the slab, and placed the sample into his mouth. His expression told me it wasn't *so* bad. He bit again, then another, until gone.

I went into the dark hut and flopped down on the crunchy mattress. As I lay thinking, I placed my hands behind my head and Sara fought her way back into my mind. I thought about what she was doing. I wondered if she worried about me. Then I thought about Scupper, and if she missed me, if her nose was pressed against the lanai door, or even if she knew I was gone. I turned onto my side and fell asleep.

*****

I awoke in darkness, my wet, sweaty shirt clinging to my chest. I laid flat briefly, staring into the flickering light coming from outside near the fire pit. Robert Dean's bed was empty. By habit, I checked my watch, which was dead.

I went to the doorway and saw the fire pit bright, and double, if not triple the size for ideal cooking. I marched through the threshold and down to it. I hadn't eaten anything all day, and my stomach knotted painfully. I snooped around the fire like a dog foraging for scraps. Then found the satchel from earlier and began chewing on cattails. Its celery texture, bitter and dry, left an aftertaste I could've done without.

I enjoyed the sovereignty while sitting next to the fire. The air had an early evening feel to it, and as I sat, the wood burned close enough to feel the heat on my legs. I removed my shirt and fanned it against the flames, sending its pungent smell into the night.

The flames dried my shirt in a matter of minutes but before placing it back on, I gripped the fish emblem necklace in the palm of my hand and studied it. I'd been wearing it the entire time and the quarter-sized fish was no longer the white bone it had been a couple days prior. I blew into it trying to clear the dirt and grime that filled the tiny slits for gills. Then I put my warm shirt back on.

I sat at the fire and thought again how nice it would be to have Sara next to me. Not seeing her these couple days only grew my affection for her. How nice it would be to be in my basin loafing atop the houseboat, watching the sunset. I wondered again about Scupper, if she was getting along with Sara's parents' dog. The more I thought, the more I grew excited for myself and Robert Dean's escape later tonight—I was ready to return to my simple life.

Footsteps on shells interrupted my thoughts. I saw no one anywhere, including down the dark, moonlit path. The sounds increased, unmistakable footsteps—not animal but had the momentum of human. I checked both directions, only to hear the crunching of shells. "What is going on?" I murmured.

Still sitting, I searched for movement at the hut next to ours—nothing, but I still heard the eerie crunch of oyster shells. I stuck a finger in my ear to clear it.

Suddenly, a hand slapped on my back, a near stoppage of my heart—then a voice: "Got yah."

"Damn, man. You scared the crap out of me."

Robert Dean smiled, and onto the tree stump bench, sat next to me.

I peeked around nervously. "Where were you?"

My friend reached into an overall pocket, pulled out a clear half-filled mason jar.

"Here, take this." He handed me the jar.

"You didn't…?"

"Sure did," he said.

"You snuck back to the houseboat?"

"Yes, sir."

"Did you see it guarded?"

"Nope," he replied with a sly smirk.

"This news is good to hear." I cracked the lid and sniffed. "This smells like high-octane fuel."

Robert Dean noticed the green palm frond satchel lying near my feet and reached for it. He peeked inside the dark pouch, then dropped it back to my feet.

"Here, have these." He reached into another pocket and handed me a can of beans and a protein bar.

"Oh, nice."

He checked his back. "Enjoy, those are the last of 'em."

I pulled on the ring and poured the beans into my mouth. "I can't thank you enough," I said, chewing. "I had to eat cattails." The rich texture and the soft squish of bean hijacked my taste buds. "You couldn't grab the seasoning?" I said, grinning and chewing.

"I sure looked for it, but you must've hid it."

I continued to chew while he watched patiently, then dug out the seasoning from his pocket.

"Here," he said.

"Cool, you did bring it. It'll make a huge difference."

"You ain't kiddin'," he said.

I sprinkled a few shakes on the remaining beans left in the can.

"Easy now," he said.

I finished and handed the seasoning to him. "How long did I sleep?"

"Few hours—at least."

I scratched my head. "Hmf…"

"Yup."

"How did you sneak off to the houseboat?"

"Easily … I snuck on."

"No, serious. Snuck on? How?"

"Well, I sat 'round here while you were sleepin' and noticed everyone streamin' toward the center of this place so, since your buddy wasn't 'round, I went to check things out. Next thin' I know I was real close to the houseboat—too close not to check it out. So, I went to investigate. You know, recon. I had to wait a few minutes. The guard didn't seem to be payin' too close attention, but he *was* there. I waited and watched while he glared at the bright glow from the fire illuminating above the high pines. Eventually, he wandered off far enough so I could sneak awn in … that's it."

"What did you see, in the center?"

"I'm not sure, but it looked like a good ol' party and what-not. People sang and danced. Massive bonfire burnin', too."

I suggested, "Maybe we should change our plan to sooner rather than later."

"I'm not so sure, Shamus. He was close enough to hear if we started the engines."

"We wait until much later then."

I finished the protein bar and tossed the wrapper into the spitting fire. It caught, burned a blue flame, spiraled black smoke, departing into nothingness.

Robert Dean held the jar of apple pie, twisted off the top, drank a shot-sized amount, wiped his mouth on his bare sleeve, and handed the jar to me.

"Here, take some."

"My pleasure." I took the jar and drank from it. After I coughed, I added, "Strong."

"It sure is. Had a buddy brew this very jar up on his property. He's got his own backwoods brewery."

My inflamed throat made talking difficult. "Good, give my compliments to the brewer."

We drank most of what remained. Minutes later, we both had quite the buzz, and I tried to stand.

"Not yet, bubba," my friend so graciously warned.

I wobbled back to my butt and settled into a comfortable buzz. "You know what I could use right now?"

"I sure do," replied Robert Dean, stretching out the bag of cannabis I'd stowed on the boat. He unrolled the baggie and shook the contents. "Here yah go."

I opened it and smelled the buds.

"Well, let's get to it," he said.

"Sounds good to me," I replied, and faced him.

He stared. "Whenever you're good 'en ready."

Through the bag, I pressed on one of the buds, feeling it between my thumb and index finger. "I'm ready."

"Me too. Goin' be good to let the *mind* do a bit of vacationin'."

"Yeah," I replied. "I'd say it's exactly what we need."

"No doubt."

We became pleasant and relaxed, almost happy.

I asked, "You want the first hit?"

"Nah, you go ahead … you deserve it."

"Appreciate it," I replied.

Robert Dean smirked as if waiting for something.

I reached out my hand.

"What?" my friend asked.

"What do you mean, what?"

"I mean, what's the hand for?" he asked.

"Seriously, let's get to it."

"What's the hand for?" he said, smiling.

"It's out for the papers. You did grab the papers, right?"

"Oh, sure, got 'em right here." He reached into one overall pocket, then the other, then the front.

"You forgot them, huh?"

His chin dropped to his chest in defeat. "Maybe so."

"They were right next to the bag—in the compartment."

"Oops."

"What are we going to use to burn these?"

Robert Dean shuffled around on his feet. "Well, could be somethin' 'round here."

"I hope so."

"Me too."

My positive vibe came through in my voice. "I'm sure these people have devices to smoke."

"Why not go ask one of them," Robert Dean said, jerking his thumb toward the dark path. Maybe your buddy?"

"Funny. I've seen the way he handles beer. Not sure adding this is smart." I used a stick to arbitrarily stoke the fire.

Robert Dean disappeared into the hut.

I found the cooking limestone block and, using the stick, nudged half into the hot coals. It absorbed the heat with rapid intensity, and the charred meat residue from the earlier cook began sending sizzle into the air. Through one eye, I saw the fire.

Robert Dean exited the hut and sat next to me.

"Anything?" I asked.

"Not a flippin' thing."

For a few minutes we sat in silence—both wearing our thinking caps.

I glanced at the smoldering coal. "We're already halfway there. I mean … we've got the fire."

"This is true," replied my friend, nodding.

"All we got to do is figure out a way to contain just the smallest nugget, then ignite it."

"Yes, I know…"

I held the bag in my hand, and using the marble-sized buds, attempted to draw out some inspiration. "I've got it!"

"Oh?"

"Worth a shot," I replied, and held the poking stick—then nudged the limestone block away from the immediate fire. I made a stumbling lap around the fire pit, combing the ground.

"What yah looking for?"

I didn't look up, kept searching the ground. "Here we go." I picked up an old shard of limestone and hurried back next to Robert Dean and sat.

"What's that for?"

"It's a small piece of an old cooking stone. I think if we heat it up, it might cook the cannabis."

"Really?"

"If we can get it hot enough, which I think we can, it will ignite the small buds!"

"Then what?"

I simulated sipping through a straw. "Then we breathe in the smoke, see?"

"Ain't goin' work," he said.

"Why not?"

"Because…" Robert Dean's voice slurred.

I knelt next to the hot coals and placed the playing card-sized shard on top. "This shouldn't take long to heat."

"Now, how we gonna pick it up when it's hot, huh?"

"Using this," I replied, holding the nudge stick.

"Shamus, I'm tellin' you, it *ain't* goin' work."

I didn't answer and surveyed the shard, hopeful for a quick heat-up.

Robert Dean checked the trail.

"All clear?" I asked as though us getting caught with the cannabis would render some sort of primal punishment.

"Seems like it," he replied, and reached for the mason jar. He held it up to the fire's light.

"Anything?"

"Nope, she's a-empty."

The night's quietness became weird, hearing multiple crackles and quick whistles when the fire unsealed wooden air pockets.

"Is that thing ready to go?" Robert Dean said.

"Let me check."

I nudged the shard from the hot coals and slid it to a clear patch of dirt. I licked my fingertips and gingerly touched the surface. It felt hot, but not hot enough to start the cannabis. "It's not quite hot enough."

"Told you, it ain't goin' work."

I muttered, "Maybe not, but at least I'm trying."

Robert Dean held the tin lid from the bean can and began manipulating it, thumbs depressing the center while holding it against his chest. The tin lid popped as it bent. He held it to the firelight to check the progress. Satisfied, he lowered it against his chest and began rolling it up like a tiny newspaper.

"Ain't going to work," I said.

"Ain't goin' work? Trust me, it will work fine. Always had before."

"Before when?" I asked.

"Before before."

"You're weird," I said.

I lowered my eyes to the limestone shard resting on the smooth patch of dirt near my feet and tried to focus. The fast-approaching stupor clouded my vision. I told Robert Dean, "I imagined the shard acting as if it were a kitchen stovetop on high heat. All one needs to do is spill an uncooked noodle on the element to see what I was getting at."

My friend answered, "I know."

"You do?" My words slurred. "When? Before?"

"Sure did. Where else would you have gotten that silly idea?"

"Silly?"

"Yes."

I grinned. "I would have worked just fine if I gave it more time. Put a bit more effort into it."

Robert Dean had the tin lid folded in the same shape as a nicely rolled cigarette. He leaned it close to the firelight to inspect his modification.

I sat to his right, said, "Why not go—no—*sneak* back to the houseboat, okay? Get an empty beer can. That's an easy and rather quick way to smoke the cannabis, no?"

"I ain't goin' back—not right now anyways."

"Why not?"

"Too risky. Damn, Shamus, did you hear anythin' I said earlier? It's guarded, remember?"

"You said 'sort of guarded.'" I did remember. But the apple pie removed my internal filter, so the words spewed out filter less.

I removed my visor and scratched my head. I was tired and hadn't slept or eaten much in the last couple days. In fact, I was antsy and weak, needed carbohydrates and calories. My mind craved to know our plan was going to work. It wasn't the most well-thought-out plan, but I had to get out tonight. I wanted to leave tonight, and I was sure Robert Dean wanted out too.

"This should work just fine," Robert Dean said. He held out the bean can lid that he'd formed into a tightly rolled metal tube.

"What are we smoking, crack?"

"Funny, she'll do just fine."

"You sure?" I asked. "I don't think it's tight enough."

"Well, Shamus, I think it's tight just fine."

I handled the piece, critiqued, and pointed it to the fire to focus through the tiny hole like a telescope. Through it, a tiny smudge of light reflected into my eye. I then blew through it, and the air whistled as it left the tip. "Might work," I mumbled, handed it back to my friend, seized the bag of cannabis, and opened it. In the low light, I raised it to the fire, only seeing tiny black nuggets through the transparent bag. I selected the largest one while Robert Dean made vital last-minute adjustments to the tool.

He said, "Boy, I'll be glad to get back to the ol' houseboat and finish off our weekend in *style*."

"There might not be any time left. It's already Saturday night. Your flight leaves tomorrow night, right?"

"Monday."

"Oh."

"Yup." Robert Dean held the tool to the fire on a stick.

"Let's not decide anything, we haven't escaped yet."

"We'll make it out," he said, "I have a gooood feelin' about it."

"That makes one of us." I lifted the bud to my nose and sniffed. Its scent was hard to describe, somewhere between skunk cabbage and hops, distinct and stimulating, and the smell of new, the smell of all things possible. I finished with it and handed it to my friend. "Here, take it."

He compared the nugget's size to the tool's bowl-end. The two weren't the same. The nugget needed to be broken into smaller pieces.

"Break it up." I rose to relieve myself and stumbled to the corner of the hut where I needed to lean, but I didn't think its thin walls would support my weight. I turned toward the trail and saw a faded outline, an obscure boundary as though there wasn't a thing beyond it. "Why are we left alone?" I mumbled. The air had cooled. To guess the time, I'd say it was ten o'clock. I finished and went back to the fire, sat hard, and practically fell to the ground. I was lit, and it was obvious.

"You alright, Shamus?"

"Oh, I'm just feelin' lit."

"I can tell."

"You?"

"Somewhat—but not as lit as I'd like, ol' buddy."

"I get lit very quickly," I said.

"That apple pie is not for the weary." He sounded like, "Zat apple eye snot for dah worry." I wasn't sure if it was his slur or my ears.

"Am I weary?"

"I don't know, are you?" Robert Dean began modifying the tool, implementing a few final tweaks.

"I'm not sure," I said.

"Well, I hope the apple pie is gettin' lonely."

"Why is that?"

He peered through the little tin tube. "Because I think we're almost a-go here."

"You got it working?"

He blew through the tool. "It's quite possible."

Just the thought of adding to my current inebriation seemed almost redundant.

I flinched, thought I felt something on my shoulder. "Did you hear that?"

"Hear what?" Robert Dean replied.

"Sounded like footsteps on shells."

Robert Dean stuck his head up like a prairie dog. He swiveled to the wide path, searching the small campsite. "I think you're hearin' things, Shamus."

"I don't think so. It sounds like it's getting closer." My heart began pounding. "It's the same sound I heard earlier, right before you returned."

"Almost there," he said, focused on his task.

I rose and rotated three-hundred and sixty-degrees, probing all ways possible for the sound. Robert Dean hummed a bluegrass song as he finalized his fabrication.

"You don't hear that?" I said. "It's weird."

"Nope." He didn't look up, sang, "…and down by the river is where the grass grows a- greenest, and so the tree wins again."

"It sounds like it's getting closer and closer."

He sang more. "The trees are tall, the trees are strong, and it's because of the river…" Robert Dean ended and raised the final product. "Well, lookie here."

I ultra-focused on the crunching shells. I heard something but didn't see it. I sat back down.

Robert Dean stretched out his hand, holding the tin mold. "Here, you take the honors."

I reached for it and aligned it to my lips, sending my vision down the barrel of the tubular device. What I saw across the fire knocked me from the wooden bench.

Chapter Fifteen

I **squinted** to make sure it was real.

Three Bands appeared across the fire, his face set in stone, the sockets of his eyes swallowed in painted charcoal, so the whites flared sharp as bone. The three red armbands gripped his biceps high and tight, throbbing in the firelight. Against the blaze his skin gleamed like oiled wood. In his fist, he held the spear with unyielding strength.

I slanted my lips to the side. "Robert Dean," I whispered.

He hadn't noticed, and at arm's length held out the tool. "Go ahead, now. Take'er first."

I kept stone still and used my eyes to direct his attention across the fire.

He turned and his confounded expression turned back to me. "How? What?"

"I *told* you I heard something."

He faced the fire, whispered, "He a sneaky sonovabitch."

"That's what *I'm* saying…"

My friend cupped the tool and eased it down his overalls' pocket using an index finger—out of sight. "He looks meaner than he did before, no?"

"Does, yes."

I leered at Three Bands with one eye shut. My attempt to stabilize and align the three images down to one proved futile. His mouth didn't move but I heard words.

"He wants to take us," I said.

"How do you figure?" Robert Dean replied.

"You didn't hear that?"

"Hear what?"

I nodded to Three Bands. "Him."

"What's up with your hearin', Shamus?" he whispered. "When we's get back to the civilized world, I think you ought'n get your ears checked—"

"*Carjama geeto muna.*"

Robert Dean froze. "Um…"

I initiated a stare-down into Three Bands' eyes. He broke, orbited around the fire, and arrived feet from us. Spear raised, he said again, "*Carjama geeto muna.*"

I said, "I'm pretty sure that means "let's go" or something related."

Robert Dean rolled to his feet, brushed off his overalls, said, "I bet I know where we're goin'."

The walk was harsh. Momentum carried me heavy-footed as Three Bands led Robert Dean and I to the center of the community, where people danced and gathered in the shadows of the trails.

Though the hour was late, the night itself felt strangely new—alive in a way that unsettled me. The air carried a vibrancy that made the darkness seem young, unfinished, as if the evening had only just begun. Last night had been muted and dull, but tonight pulsed with the unmistakable sense that it was far from over.

Robert Dean didn't stumble and harbored no stupor. He walked like Three Bands, as though on a moving sidewalk.

Dark palm tree silhouettes developed out of nowhere. I walked in a clear line as they emerged in random, tracking Three Bands while he led us. He didn't walk behind us in his normal position, but ahead, instructing us to follow. He also didn't deviate from his walking line, even though trees and palmettos blocked his path.

After maybe a mile, the light of a whipping fire came into view. Through smoke plume clouds were the bright tops of slash pines and sable palms. Their chants echoed and pinged off trees, stinging into my brain.

Robert Dean was on my left side, hands balled into fists, now swaying for balance.

I gazed upward at the bright clearness of the cloudless night sky, where visible stars appeared through the breaks in the brush. The smell of smoke filled the air when we arrived at the pulsing heart of the village, where the sounds of whispers and private conversations swept through the haze. Chief's mansion hulked in silence off to the side, near a two-story bonfire.

Groups of villagers had formed tight rings around the fire, lining up in rows, and dancing clockwise. Kids skipped and jumped while attached to their mother's tight hand. A methodical placement of benches made from cabbage palm stumps edged along the fringe. Grouping of villagers occupied them while others sat on the shell ground.

The thick, shelled earth beneath my feet also had an interesting effect on the cacophony of sounds. The loud, constant crunch of shell controlled me as it resonated in different areas off the surrounding trees.

The walk had given my mind good reason to stay cognizant, resulting in a moderately, or so I thought, sober appearance.

Three Bands brought us to a row of stumps and pointed us to sit. The closeness of the fire made the heat unbearable. Three Bands disappeared.

Robert Dean and I sat for minutes in silence.

The villagers moved with purpose around the fire while we sat watching. Some beat drums slung from straps around their necks, the rhythm steady and distinctive. When the train of dancers passed us, the drumming faded, only to return a short time later, circling back like the little trains in a shopping mall. At the head of the procession was a group I recognized—the same people who had led the burial ceremony that afternoon.

What Robert Dean and I were witnessing, to the best of my knowledge, might have been a ceremony for the dead—less of a dim reception, but like an afterlife afterparty. They shed no tears, just sounds of laughter and joy.

Robert Dean didn't seem to be analyzing or learning what we were experiencing.

I turned and said, "Pretty interesting, huh?"

"Yeah, it's not too bad. Nice fire."

I agreed and enjoyed the fire's flame. It ripped and sparked two stories high like a vertical orange flag whipping up into the night—flames spitting sparks, carrying embers across the entire center.

"I guess they're not worried about startin' a forest fire," Robert Dean said.

"I guess not."

He leaned to my ear. "What I don't understand is this: How come some fisherman out in the Myakka here ain't seen this fire, or even someone back in town? It sure is close enough. The smoke has to be drifting across the entire harbor. Do you think nobody can smell that?"

"I'm not sure."

He added, "I mean, I know a plane could spot it from above, no?"

"No, I agree with you—a plane for sure."

He removed the tool in a clench, then to his lips as if the answers found refuge inside, only requiring a flame to release them. "You'd think firemen would be all over this," he said, as he drew in air.

I had no reasonable answer or reply for my friend. I didn't know how these villagers had remained hidden away living this secret lifestyle for as long as they had. But they were, and that was a fact.

On the balcony of the Chief's second story mansion, four people stood. Chief's spear commanded out to the crowd while jawing, maybe to inspire, but no voice reached us. He stood in an influential pose, chin up, eyes wide, jaw clenched, confident in movement as any leader should. Wife, strong by his side, maybe a church parishioner, eyes closed, hands up and forward, though she could feel the fire from her height.

I pointed Robert Dean to what I witnessed. "See that?"

"I do."

"Cool, no?"

"We should be up there in the VIP section instead of out here feeding the damn mosquitoes." He then swatted across his face and smacked his neck.

"They're bad, I know. Should have brought the bug spray, and the seasoning."

Prior to Robert Dean mentioning the furious attacking mosquitoes, not one of those bloodsuckers had landed on me—not bitten once. Now that he'd brought it to the center of the conversation, all I could focus on was the irritating buzzing around my face. I swatted repeatedly but couldn't seem to shake them. I stood rapidly, staggering closer to the fire nearly encroaching into the settlers dancing past like a human chain-link fence. I again shook and swatted. Still, the bloodsuckers landed readily with full bodily coverage, attacking my legs, arms, head, feet, and ears. The hood of my fishing shirt provided little protection as they seemed to be eating through it. I hurried to Robert Dean sitting pleasantly on the stumps with the fire glow lighting his face.

"What's the matter with you, Shamus? Has your chicken flown the coup?"

"These mosquitoes, they bite and bite hard."

He laughed at my panicking.

I made it to a point where I'd defeated the bastards, or so thought, and sat, and when I did, fell over.

"You alright?" Robert Dean asked.

"I'm fine. It's just these damn flesh-eating insects. I can't seem to shake them."

"That's weird, because they seem to have quit bitin' me altogether."

I rose again, removed my hooded fishing shirt, began scratching my arms, and decided to approach the flames of the fire to burn the little devils off my skin. The hot rays were warm and had no effect on the mosquito's rampage. To reach my backside, I slung an arm behind my shoulder and pushed at the elbow, to reach the rarest parts of my spine. The fish medallion shone white in the firelight. I pressed it between my fingers, praying for some relief as I stumbled back to my friend.

Robert Dean had the tool held forward. "I think you need to take this, Shamus. You've come unglued."

"Unglued? I think these bugs have an agenda."

He grinned. "The agenda is to survive."

"They will survive well—on me."

"Everythin's got to eat. Nothing new there," my friend countered.

"You sound like me." My shirt went back on as I sat. "We need to get to the boats as soon as humanly possible and get out of here."

"Funny…" he said.

"What?"

"You," he said.

"Me?"

"Yes."

"Why is that funny?" I asked.

"Because."

"Because why?"

He slapped his knee. "You get bit by a few mosquitoes and all of a sudden you're wantin' to leave?"

"I've been wanting to leave…"

"Not like this."

"You figure this how?" I asked.

He turned to face me. "This is the first time I've heard you wantin' to leave."

I stood again. "Okay, you try being tortured by tiny no-see-ums and swarms of mosquitoes."

He scoffed. "I've been bitten plenty, trust me."

"Not like this. I wouldn't wish this on my worst enemy. Let's go."

Robert Dean coughed and faced behind me. "Great, just when I was beginning to enjoy m'self."

I whipped around, saw Three Bands lurking behind us. I could do nothing more than stand tall and face him, which I did, and lurched forward. His juke of my drunken stumble was effortless for him. The spear was nowhere in sight, but he gripped something in his right hand, which at one point might have breathed air.

"Gator." Robert Dean noted.

Three Bands removed a torch size branch from alongside the fire, dipped it into the flames, and brought it to the area where we sat. He laid the gator tail across the fiery branch. Its putrid skin began to smoke.

After seconds, Three Bands removed the sizzling, fetid gator tail and swung it like a lasso. Smoked spiraled as the tail whirled and cooled. Once he spun the tail a dozen revolutions, he tested the tail's smokey skin, where the white flesh had become exposed. He seemed satisfied and trooped back to us.

Robert Dean leaned to me and said, "Repellent."

"Huh?"

Three Bands demonstrated by wiping a fleshy chunk of gator fat from the tail onto his arm. Then using fingers, he nipped at the air, slapped his arm, and pointed at me.

"I see now." I raised my sleeve and reached out my hand.

He tore a golf ball-sized chunk off the tail. I took the warm offering, wiped it on my skin, releasing the grease that left behind a squalid layer of film. The aromatic rankness brought up a strident gag. I repeated the procedure on my neck and legs.

"Your turn, bubba," I said to Robert Dean.

He shook his head, held up a hand. "Oh no. I'm doin' just fine, thanks."

Three Bands' slighted mannerisms were all Robert Dean needed to agree, and he rose, stomped forward, and reached for a smoking chunk of flesh.

"Fine," he said, holding up the piece of flesh. "Happy?"

"Don't be too miffed," I said. "It's actually working,"

He eased it toward his hairy forearm. "I'm sure it shall."

I breathed in the rancid stench from my arm. "Smells of the worst possible thing, though."

Robert Dean smeared a thin coat on his left arm, and with a fulfilled obligation, handed the remaining piece back to Three Bands, who didn't take it, but drifted away, fading into the dark side of the fire.

"It really does seem to be working," I said, examining my legs.

"Well, it smells like death and I'm gettin' it off." My friend stumbled behind our stumps, found a pile of crumpled leaves, and began to wipe his arm.

"It's not that bad," I said.

"Maybe for you."

"I'd rather use it than get mauled by these tiny killers."

"I'd rather keep what little food I have in my stomach … where it is, and not on the ground."

"For someone who deals in the smells you do on a daily basis, you sure seem to be quite sensitive."

"Agreed, but only on rare occasions do I smear the work across my skin."

"Good point."

Robert Dean smiled and sat.

We continued watching the villagers enjoying the festal night. The train of people dancing around the roaring fire had swelled while, from every shadow, jubilant villagers continually joined, leaping off their benches, skipping to the fire, walking hand in hand.

"Here already," Robert Dean said, waving, extending the tool and the small stick from a lit branch to light the cannabis.

"It works?" I asked.

To prove to me it did, my friend exhaled a plume of blue smoke, filling the surrounding area in a translucent cloud, hand lifting to his mouth as he tried to mute a cough through a clenched fist. After the sampling, I too, was forced to cough.

"Harsh," I said, coughing through my fist.

"You felt that too?"

"I did."

"Hurts, right?"

"Little." I handed the tool to my friend.

He went for a second round, and tempted me with another, but I didn't take.

I wanted to test the apple pie's compatibility alongside the cannabis. In this very moment in time, it wasn't in me to rush. The two, and their effects, had to reach an agreement before I would proceed. It took a long moment for a decision to be made.

Suddenly, a buzz covered me like a soothing mental trench coat, protection from the inconsistencies of the outside. Like a warm layer of fuzz, the emotional gamut I underwent appeared clearly on my face—I smiled.

The large fire smoldered, intensifying, wafting the smoke high into the tips of the pines.

While my body drew heavy, my mind became light, lucid. Through my inner eyes, I'd been lifted and given a much more vivid view of my surroundings.

Ahead of me, the villagers had swollen to hundreds of people, prancing gaily, elbows linked with a level of mental detachment from anything resembling modern reality. I was safe on the assumption that they didn't know about molecules, or atoms, and might never have had the thirst for such knowledge. They didn't contemplate experimental physics or ponder over math theory. There were no signs they had found religion other than a minuscule flicker of a possible deity, yet they went on surviving, living in each moment so profound it was contagious. They went on dancing as though nothing else mattered. So far, I'd witnessed no competition, no envy or greed. All was one in the village with an abundance of harmony.

My sight trailed as I swung my head to face Robert Dean.

He sat holding the tool to his lips—saw me and asked, "You want another one or what? It's about cashed."

I reached for the rolled-up bean can lid in silence, set it to my mo81uth, and stretched for the lit twig. But before igniting, something compelled me to lift my eyes from the tool, and to the line of dancing villagers. From two layers deep, I saw her.

Chapter Sixteen

Her eyes pointed at me as she strode touchless through the mob of people. Her black hair, dark as a crow's feather, parted along each side of a topless torso. She stepped lightly and slowly, and she conducted herself as though the party was all hers. Her face had a sharp, symmetrical nose and thin beige lips—neck was brown, cylindrical, and it hung a medallion similar to mine.

Robert Dean sniffed his arm where he'd applied the gator grease.

"Psst," I said.

He made no move.

"Hey, you seeing this?" I asked.

Robert Dean continued focusing on his sappy forearm without a flicker of acknowledgment.

The woman remained deep in form, danced hard, seemed to move in slow motion—head back, eyes closed, arms out, and using movement, explained how to live. I couldn't pry my eyes off her. I could feel what *she* felt. She had natural beauty—mesmerizing dark-toned skin. With side-sweeping hips, she bent forward, and her neck rolled counter-clockwise—a vociferous upward snapping head trailed straight hair that formed a black arc.

Villagers danced and swept past her as though she wasn't there. But she *was* there, she was *very* there.

Her suggestive moves synchronized with the beat of the drums. Several villagers danced nearby but weren't dancing with her. No one could dance with her. She had untouchable motion.

The woman I envied demanded all of me. Her insinuated demands were that I give her all that I had—a depletion of emotions. I wanted to give her three times what I could afford; and because of her I would become emotionally bankrupt.

Her eyes sprang open into a hypnotic glow of emerald green. I tried to break away, but she engrossed me to the point of incoherence.

Visions of Sara flashed into my head. Sara's smile, a feather of hair blocking her eye as she pulled me into her arms and down onto grass green under a royal palm trunk. They were at war with the woman and her trance. "Shamus, what am I going to do with you?" I heard Sara say as she loved me.

The magnetic trance of the woman in the village called to me, and I lifted from the seat while she zapped me into an emotionally enamored state, pulling me in her cerebral tractor beam. Her mind summoned me into an ocular trap, and I went as though I hadn't taken a single step.

To stand next to her was euphoric. A hand reached out and touched my arm—a touch so gently that if I hadn't been watching it, I might not have felt it at all. It started on my bicep, and as she pulled me, slid down to my elbow onto my wrist, and finally to my fingertips. Once she broke touch, the addiction was real, and I wanted more.

I was close enough to speak. Our fingers remained inched apart. She lived in the space precisely before untouched and touched, and she couldn't have lived more than twenty years.

As we rotated on the fringe of the massive fire, we passed benches filled with people. I had yet to experience the opposing side of the two-story fire, so I fought to look.

We went on as though she pulled me along attached to an imaginary leash—a leash I wanted to be on. I saw, as we danced, a large grouping of villagers on the fire's opposite side from where we had begun. Chief and his associates danced among them, having moved down to ground level. Chief was waving his staff.

I tried to wave, but they didn't respond.

Three Bands held the spear now and pointed it toward the sky as he mouthed to the same melody as the chanting. I told myself to let go, to fall into the night.

She released me from her mental leash, and I moved solo, faster, to gain another inch on her, but couldn't as she became the prey. I couldn't run faster. Every inch I gained, she became the same inch farther. I didn't wonder where she led me, only that if I would catch her. I wanted to catch her. I needed to catch her.

We circled back to the side where Robert Dean sat, and I attempted to gather his attention, but he wouldn't look up.

Happiness carried me. I made repeated attempts to catch the crowd's attention. We went on, and I removed my shirt, skipping along, chasing the woman—my hand clenching the shirt, spinning it like a jovial toss of a grappling hook.

The gray-hooded fishing shirt didn't make it anywhere near the direction I had intended it to go. It fluttered into the air, made a boomerang right hook, rose atypical above our heads, diving into the fire like a moth to a flame. I wasn't happy to see it go, for now I was shirtless, but a lesson in merriment was worth the loss.

I turned back to the woman. Her head tilted, throat bared to the night, her arm reaching toward me with defiance. I stepped closer and nicked the tip of her middle finger. She fixed her eyes on mine—unyielding, relentless—and in that unbroken stare I felt it again, the pull of something raw and electric, a power that threatened to swallow me whole. She noticed my shirt missing and her smile deepened.

She faced me fully exposing a bare chest; erect nipples pointed toward the stars; straight black hair no longer covered them. She moved closer and touched my shoulder.

I didn't resist.

Her eyes were on mine. She spoke to me, "To him, I am sorry." Her words sounded as though she said them down the center of an empty glass bottle.

Her hands held each one of my shoulders, and beginning at my head, gazed down. And at my necklace, her eyes searched no further, and the effervescence in her smile switched to a timorous frown. I couldn't breathe. After she touched her necklace, but scowled at mine, she screamed across the camp's wide-openness, echoing through the trees. All activity ceased, and all focus rained on me.

"Shit!" I mumbled.

Her eyes blinked from emerald to black and her smile vanished. Her splendor disappeared fast as a lightning strike; the weightlessness ended; her hair no longer hovered in thin air. The glimmering vibe was gone.

Aggressive attention paralyzed me as I remained still with what seemed like hundreds of eyes pressing on my skin like tiny piercing needles.

I turned to face the now heatless fire that had shrunk to just one red ember.

I faced the woman again, and now within a few inches of my face, heard the word, "Run." Its clarity rang out, and I froze in pure shock. My breath went shallow; I shook my head, forcing air back into my lungs. My eyes swept the crowd of onlookers; their anger fixed on me. The girl had disappeared.

The full release of the trance was emotionally stressful. I did the one thing left and began walking toward the opposite side of the fire, where Robert Dean sat.

The entire village, including Chief, followed me like a gang of the undead.

I realized I was in deep trouble.

Urgency pressed against me as I closed in on Robert Dean's bench. When his shape surfaced through the dark, I lengthened my stride, fighting the instinct to break into a run—knowing the sudden burst might spark a chase.

Robert Dean was sitting in the same spot on the stumps muddling with the same yellow greasy stain on his arm. He didn't acknowledge when I approached and murmured once I reached inside twenty feet. He was nearly unresponsive. Behind me, the crowd closed in like the shelf cloud of an approaching cold front.

"Hey," I said. "Hey!"

I slid into the stumps and tried verbally to regain his attention. But nothing. I shook his shoulder. "Robert Dean? Bud? Look!"

His focus left his arm and faced up to me—eyes that shone glazed three times over. His mouth sagged, lips dripped drool.

"This can't be happening," I mumbled.

I shook him like the trunk of a grapefruit tree, and the high-hung grapefruit was his consciousness. "What's gotten into you?"

Down near his feet lay the empty tool. I left it and shook him once more.

"Let's go," I said.

Through his pupils, the smoldering fire reflected on me. I shook again. This time I got the grapefruit.

"Shamus," he mumbled. "Is that you?"

I checked the crowd. "Listen, bud … um … we gotta get going."

I reached under his armpit and lifted but due to his weight, I couldn't get any sensible leverage. I had to raise his arm behind my neck and across my shoulder, then hoist. His bulk needed all my strength to lift even an inch off the bench. I quickly realized that this wasn't going to get us far.

"I need you to snap out of it. Time to go."

"Go?" he said weakly.

"Yes, go."

His head rolled to face me. "But we just got here. I was just gettin' warmed up."

I failed in pathetic fashion to stabilize Robert Dean's weight enough to take a single step. It was no use to continue. The impossibility of making a run for it soon appeared; the villagers had gained too much ground.

Robert Dean slowly came around. "Hey, where'd your shirt go?"

"Blown into the fire. I'll tell you about it later."

Robert Dean concurred.

I nodded toward the angry mob. "We have a bigger problem at the moment."

My friend laughed as though nothing else was happening. "Oh, yeah, what's that, Shamus?" Once finished, his head rolled drunkenly toward the fire; saw for himself. "Ho-ley sheep shit!"

"Yeah," I said.

"What have you done now?" His coherence grew.

The villagers closed in enough that only a whisper would conceal our voices. I said from the corner of my mouth, "I think this…" I handled my necklace. "…is somewhat of an issue."

"Oh? It is, is it?"

The whole group was present. Chief stood strong, heading up his clan, and wife by his side. Three Bands arrived as well, crept to our flank, embracing the spear in attack position.

Robert Dean tried to stand on his own. "This *can't* be good."

Groups of aggressive, wide-eyed villagers surrounded us completely. If we tried to escape, we would lose, because to break free would force us to penetrate multiple layers of people.

I released my friend's weight back onto the stumps and straightened my spine to appear as a formidable opponent. Standing in silence, the circle of villagers wore frightening, malicious grins, unopen to discussion. But Chief's trenchant eyes were no match. I knew I had done something wrong— knew it must be about the beyond-beautiful woman, and or the tiny fish emblem nestled between my pectoral muscles.

Chief's arm extended, gripping the staff, then dug it in like a skier before taking a run. After the first dig, he paused and made another in the same way. He revealed the anger in his mind as his dark, red-painted eyes slanted. He stepped forward, eyes beaming on the charm. "This is the token of great tragedy and must not be owned. Embracing the token attributes death."

My mouth dropped. "Umm…"

He raised his staff toward the south. "I sent it to the beyond and never to be found."

"Ahh…" I turned toward Robert Dean for support, who only shrugged and stood oblivious. I turned back toward Chief said in a studder. "I—I f-found it over near the Pirate Harbor area—" I pointed, paused, tried to gather some wits. After a deep breath, said, "I mean south … next to the … *GREAT* mangrove wall."

He followed my finger.

I whispered to Robert Dean, "How's he now speaking English?"

"English? All I hear is that mumbo jumbo tribal talk."

That struck me as surprising. Robert Dean, now so far inebriated he couldn't understand English?

Chief stepped to within arm's length.

"Here," I said, and reached for the boned fish and yanked, breaking the clasp. I held it out for him. "Take it. As a gift." I bowed. "I have no need for it."

The crowd let out a strident, simultaneous gasp.

Chief leaned back, slanted one eye, blinked, reacting to the crowd—voice was deep, gruff, and the words were clearer than the Florida sky after a winter's front: "You may *not* discard here! He who embraces the token attributes death!"

I frowned. "Yeah, I got that part," I mumbled.

"What's he sayin'?" asked Robert Dean.

"He says whoever holds this thing is in deep shit, basically."

"Great…"

I said Chief's way, "Well, we've been here for a couple days, and we've caused no death, so…"

"Not yet you have not," Chief said. "But it will come quick."

"Whose death?"

He extended the staff. "You, the one who embraced the token."

"Perfect…" I muttered.

He added, "And all who befriends you." His chin rose. "The punishment is death by moon."

"Death by moon?" I curled my brow in a skeptical manner. "What the hell is that?"

He slung his staff toward the sky. "It is said that he who dies by moon comes back to life as any creature, of lesser value, that only he chooses."

I decided to play along. "I'm sure we can work something out. I found it buried in a clump of oysters—thought it to be interesting and decided to hold it temporarily, really."

His eyes said that he had no time for games. "He who embraced the token attributes death!"

"Death by moon?" My brain couldn't make any sense. "What does that *even* mean?"

He kept talking. "You will not *feel* pain, you will not *know* pain, but you will *meet* death,

as *will* all."

"Jesus, that's comforting…" I mumbled.

Robert Dean whispered frantically, "We should have left when we had the chance."

Three Bands loitered ten feet to my right, waiting for something, maybe the go-ahead from Chief to slice our heads off.

The eyes of Chief's wife became moist as tears dripped. Her head shook in disbelief—upset at what I'd done. If one didn't know better it would appear though we had committed a crime, and to the best of my knowledge, we hadn't.

I kept the necklace tight in my fist. Seeing the anger on the villagers' faces gave me an urge to run—to sprint toward the fire and spike the necklace into the burning flames.

I asked Chief, "How is it that now you speak and understand my words?"

"Words…" He raised his chin, "we have always understood, and have known the language the pale one speaks from the day you appeared at the beach … onto *our* land."

"But why *now* do you understand?" I repeated.

Chief cleared his throat. "I should ask of you that question. We have always spoken

and always heard."

By studying Three Bands' mannerisms, and from his stature, procuring support wasn't happening because he too, had tears in his eyes. The spear shuddered in his grip. Unto his scowling eyes, twitching lips, and wrinkled forehead, there was more pain in him than one man should ever bear. He wanted to kill us right there and now.

The crowd began to tighten around us. Like savages, they wanted to tear us apart. Time was slipping away, a loss of hope, but then I thought about the girl.

"Who is the girl?"

By the crowd's stunned reaction, my words they now understood, and spoke in eerie unison, "Embracing the token attributes certain death."

I mumbled, "I got that part."

Robert Dean turned my way. "What in the—"

I cast a concerning stare across the first layer of people, figured if I could win them over, we'd have the best chance for freedom. "Listen…" I began. "I have given you food. I have given you tools. Does this not count for anything?"

"The power of the necklace is too great for this life," Chief said. "It brings pain and suffering. It cannot go unseen."

"What power are you referring to? Because I've held it for some time, and I've attributed *no* death and triggered *no* pain."

"You do not understand," Chief said, spiking his spear. "You cannot live with it here. It has been cursed."

"Cursed?"

"I sent it away long ago and should not have been found."

"But it is found, see?" I held it out.

Chief grudgingly allowed the crowd another reaction, then said, "You do not understand. You cannot live with it here. It's been cursed."

I said, eyeing the token in my hand. "If you say so. But it feels just like a normal object to me…"

Chief noted the quiet crowd, then said to me, "What it feels to you is of no importance to me or my people."

"But I'm trying to prove to you of its harmlessness."

"It is harmless when it is not found. It now has been found and brought back, and will attribute death to he who embraced it."

"Here," I said frustratingly. "Let me toss it into the fire." I made for a step forward, but Three Bands blocked me. "You get it, right?" I said to him. "Listen, all we have to do is take the boat and we'll get rid of it, and you'll never see us again." I looked at Robert Dean. "Right?"

"Sure as shit won't…" he said, nodding rapidly.

I turned to Chief. "See … no more problem … all solved."

"Problem will only be solved when he who embraced the token is passed through the portal of life to the other side. Then my people will rest."

"There's got to be—"

Chief lowered the spear and dropped his tone to a debate level. "There is one thing, of many, that my people can do for you since, I do believe, and have been told, that people who wear the pale skin are decent from time to time."

"We are … really," I said to Chief, then turned to Three Bands. "We mean no harm." I pressed my hands together as if to pray.

"This is what I believe, and have been told," Chief said. "So, for this, I grant you a quick death."

"What he sayin'?" my friend asked.

"He says he likes us and has an offer for us."

"What kind of offer?"

"Not sure yet."

"Not sure?"

"Well, he says that he's offering us a quick death because he likes us."

Robert Dean, whose head was shaking, rose abruptly, and presenting a clenched fist, leaned to take a step toward Chief's wife. "Time I take a stab at it."

Three Bands intercepted and swung the spear. It cracked atop Robert Dean's head, sounding like a coconut falling on cement. He dropped.

"Was that necessary?" I knelt, rolled Robert Dean onto his back and shook his jaw, sending a wave throughout his jowls. "You all right, buddy?"

Robert Dean rubbed his head, laughing. "Unbelievable."

I stood aggressively and faced Three Bands, who crouched in attack position. "Really? Again?"

He answered, "Our people require it to stay safe."

"Stay safe?"

Three Bands' tears fell like rain. "What we know is that you have technology that can hurt us. We must stay safe."

"Why would we hurt you?"

"Why wouldn't you?" Chief countered.

Our conversation began to circle so I focused on Robert Dean. "How's the head?"

His paw of a hand pressed down on a soon-to-be goose egg. "Just peachy."

I went back to the chief and said, "What is it that's so cursed about this token, as you call it?"

"The bearer of the token brought much pain and suffering to our village."

Under my breath, I said, "Yeah, I figured that much." Now louder, "I don't understand why we can't make a deal?"

"Deal?"

"Yes, a deal. Look at what we have accomplished. You have shown us your way of living, and we have shown you useful things related to ours. You let us be witness to a death, a passing. That must have meant something?"

The chief stiffened proudly as though he'd solved a riddle. "It is well acquired, and very useful knowledge that you can take with you and pass along."

"Good, good. So, we're going be able to pass it along, and we will as soon as you let us leave?"

"You will be leaving soon, and the wisdom you have acquired will guide you on your journey through the portal of life."

Robert dean straightened his suspenders. "What's the damage?"

"Plenty … don't think this guy has a clue what I'm getting at."

"I think he knows what he's doing." Robert Dean inspected the knot forming under his hat.

I opened my hand, held out the token to my friend. "They won't tell me why this necklace is so dang evil."

Robert Dean gave me an odd look. "I don't want that thing." He blocked it with his hands, head turned away, like an upset child.

"Not you, too?"

"Well, Shamus … maybe they *are right*…"

"Right?"

"Yeah," he said. Seemed Robert Dean's mind was searching for resolution—an ending. He'd settled on the obvious.

I whispered angrily into his ear. "You can't even understand what they're saying."

Aware of our predicament, the crowd, unsettled, shifted on their feet.

Robert Dean managed one knee but succeeded to stand amid a drunken wobble. "I can understand what I need to understand. These hipster campers are afraid of that damn necklace you brought, and it looks like we're both gonna pay the price."

He swayed like a tall pine in the wind, and before he fell backward, I snagged his meaty arm and straightened him up.

I went for his ear again. "It seems so, but with you being afraid of it kind of hurts my case."

"Oh, Shamus," he said, but sounded like, *Hoe, Shuu-mas.* "You think that whatever you say will make any kind of difference right now? These people have had their flippin' way with us from the get-go."

I didn't answer.

"It ain't goin' make a single difference," he said again.

"So, you just want to give up?"

"Now, I'm not saying that at all." *Ne-ew, I'm note aying at ole.*

As we spoke, Chief's stare penetrated through my body.

His wife stood poised by his side, wiping the corner of her eyes. I didn't know whether she was upset over our demise or the story behind the token or the thought of any death brought her pain. She was hard to read, and as a woman, I would've liked her intuition toward compassion to save us, but she obviously wasn't bringing it.

Three Bands held strong to our flank.

Next came the main event.

As if on cue, the crowd shuffled, and in strode Black Mask, chest pulsing, nostrils flaring.

The man appeared much more intimidating in lower light. He stood one foot behind Chief, towering over him, and us. His body was covered in dirt, and he smelled like he'd been rolling in a pile of rotting animal carcasses. No one seemed to acknowledge it though.

I wanted to run but there was no exit—get back to my normal life on my normal little basin. I had weakened and couldn't fight them. That was a fact, so I did the first thing that came to mind.

"I can do it!" I called.

This caught them off guard.

"I can do it!" I called again.

Chief rested the spire on the ground and his eyes slanted. He was curious as to my screams.

I swept my eyes across the crowd and Black Mask. "Hear me speak!"

My words shocked them into an interested silence. They were giving me permission. Silence filled the air as every eye awaited my words. I remembered the eclipse. "I can make the sun dark," I said into their eyes.

Confusion set in across their faces.

"Good thinkin', Shamus." Robert Dean saw it too and pushed me aside. "I'll solve this *real* quick," he said, pointing toward the night sky. "The eclipse—"

I smacked his hand down. "Shhh!"

"Whaaaa—?"

"No names, man."

"Why not?"

"At least not scientific ones."

Robert Dean stood weakly, growing frustrated. "What would you like me to call it, then, Shamus?"

"I don't know. Just not that."

"Okay," he said, and pointed to the sky, directed at Chief. "You know the big bright bulb in the sky? Tomorrow we make darky, okay?"

They made no facial movement, not a muscle twitch, not an eye blink, not a shift in balance.

Robert Dean said to me, "Of all the years, you think that they've seen a blood-red solar eclipse? C'mon now…"

"It would be smart not to judge them ignorant," I said.

I recalled never seeing them measure the sky, never had they pondered the stars. They had written nothing, read nothing. All their energy went into the day-to-day—tangible tasks that had to be done. The stars seemed to play no part in their navigation; their dugout journeys rarely took them far from camp. But the moon… the moon they had to know.

"Hear me speak," I said again.

The chief raised the spire in approval.

I gazed into his eyes. "Tomorrow … I will turn the sun *dark*!"

The crowd turned their focus to themselves, mumbling, discussing my words. They understood me.

The chief said, "This is not in the realm of possibility."

"If so. If I do make the sky go dark and make the sun disappear, can we then be set free?"

Chief thought momentarily, gazed out at his crowd, grinned, and nodded. "Passing through the portal will yes, get you *free*!"

I leaned over to Robert Dean. "It's tomorrow, right? Sunday?"

"I believe you're correct. In the morning."

The lack of nutrition and water had literally zapped my strength, but I'd made my final plea. A wave of realization blanked my mind. I couldn't thwart these men. To predict the solar eclipse would be the key, the only chance of escape, so I faced up to Three Bands and attempted my final petition for repentance. "Please."

Chapter Seventeen

I sat unbalanced at the bow of an ordinary dugout canoe, placed to face forward, to sit high like a hood ornament. The stars beamed clarity through the pre-dusk darkness. A slight breeze swept over my body. I shivered, and couldn't, for the life of me, see what had become of Robert Dean. I then fell back into darkness.

The power of the apple pie created a miasmal effect on my vision, overtaking any sense of direction. I fought to sense our general route, but the continuous mind-numbing chanting of, "*Embracing the token attributes death,*" made it difficult to concentrate. If I had to guess, the canoes were taking us to the mouth of the main creek leading into the wide-open Cutoff.

Instinctually, my hand strained to paw at a throbbing contusion building itself atop my head, but they'd tied my hands behind my back, causing my shoulder muscles to painfully cramp.

*****

My next inkling of consciousness, I felt wet, and every muscle ached with twitching spasms. My head rotated from left to right, focusing on whatever sound I could find. First, I heard the soft spritz of water advancing along the side of multiple canoes—the pleasant, hypnotic, sounds of synchronized oars pressing past the water's surface, thrusting the canoe forward.

Then I heard it—the moaning, and unmistakable sound of Robert Dean's groans. I knew he sat in the canoe next to mine as the water trickled consistently along the easy-moving vessel.

As we moved along, my consciousness improved, and my clarity began to increase. After minutes had passed, I forced my eyes open and sensed the bubbling welt enlarging on the back of my cranium might be dripping blood. I made the mistake of shaking my head, and the instantaneous throbbing hit me like I'd drank a gallon of rum. After another few minutes, I faced the canoe, portside, and saw my blurry friend.

He sat in the same area of his canoe as I, but his head cocked back, mouth sagged open— he looked to be sleeping as his head rolled around like lost in a bad dream. His moaning grew, like trying to wake from a coma. I observed the canoe's pilot to be one of Three Bands' soldiers. After an indiscriminate glance toward me, he turned forward again.

Even though I couldn't move my hands, the token had found its way back, tied around my neck, a solemn indication it'd be accompanying me through the portal of life.

Although my vision was still muddy, I focused on the direction we traveled. Over the years, I'd become all too familiar with the Myakka Cutoff. I knew it better than most people did, but my visually impairment made it difficult to accurately estimate our intended destination.

Then I saw spots and began slipping, passing out. I tried to resist, but then darkness.

*****

My eyes popped open to uncontrollable shivering. Dawn was quickly approaching in the grey mist, where the gang had stretched my hands behind my back, tied to what felt like a stumped piling. Confused, I thrashed, oscillated my head, pulling at my wrists. I gained some slack, but not enough. Once settled, it was clear they had placed me sitting, tied to the piling at the head of the creek, cross-legged in water up to my shoulders.

"Well, I hope you're happy..." a familiar voice said.

Robert Dean was sitting ten feet away, also cross-legged, waist deep—arms tied behind a wooden pylon.

"What happened?" I said, then focused on the farthest parts of the Myakka Cutoff, along the distance hedges of wild mangroves. Nothing seemed abnormal. Normal tree lines consisted of dark watermarks, a few distant mullet splashes, a swooping gull, all consistent with an ordinary morning in the Myakka Cutoff.

His answer had an edge: "I guess this is how we gonna pass through the portal of life..."

I sighed. "What are we supposed to do, die from hypothermia?"

"You were passed out for, what I could guess ... an hour or so."

"That long, huh?"

"Yeee-up, and FYI, when I woke a little over an hour ago, the water was much friken lower!"

I faced the dawn sky and thought about how this simple society had figured out that the moon controlled the tides. I whispered to myself, "I guess that's what death by moon means..."

"I'm sorry?" Robert Dean asked. "Death by hwhaaat?"

"Before, at the bonfire when I was trying to get us out—"

"But you were actually makin' it worse?"

"I was trying to help."

"Oh, okay ... just checkin'."

I pushed past my friend's combative tone and said, "When we were talking, the chief said our journey through the portal of life would be by way of 'death by moon.'"

"That's funny because I thought it would've been from that crazy bastard wearin' the black mask decapitatin' us on the friggin' cold stone of death!"

"I hadn't thought much about how we are going to die, just that it seems to be imminent."

Robert Dean's false teeth rattled in his jaw. "Well, I'm glad *that* ain't happenin'."

I focused on the water at my waist. "Well, I guess we wait until the tide rises, and hope the eclipse happens before that. Right?"

"You know this eclipse gonna screw with the tides. Could make them *extra* high."

"I'm aware…"

Robert Dean's head swiveled at the sky. "Anyway, hope this eclipse shows up before the high tide. If not, we're dead as a poached snook. But in the meantime, why not work some of your magic on your lil' buddy behind yah?"

I fought to turn, to wrest even a half-rotation of my head. The effort won me only a sliver of view over my shoulder— just enough to see Three Bands standing on the narrow mangrove bank at the head of the creek where the mangrove roots under his feet knuckled into the mud like the fingers of some ancient hand. He was postured straight and stiff, like a man guarding a Queen; a spear dug in, hand resting on a well-worn grip. The sun wasn't right to make out his face, but I knew it was him.

Facing forward, I called to him. He didn't respond, but from this distance, and my awkward positioning, I couldn't tell if he acknowledged me at all. Robert Dean sat in a better position than I to make that call.

"Did he hear me?" I asked my friend.

"How would I know?" he said.

"You're in a better position. You have a better line of sight."

Robert Dean faced forward, then in aggravation, glanced toward Three Bands. "Nope, didn't see any kind of reaction."

"You sure?

"Does it really matter, Shamus… At. This. Point. In. Time?"

"It might. You just asked me to talk to him."

"I did indeed, but really, what? You goin' try some secret language and talk us out of here? C'mon…"

"Something like that," I muttered. "You wanted me to try some magic on him…"

Robert Dean head faced forward as though he was done talking to me.

I shifted, called to Three Bands in hopes of reminding him of the hospitality I'd shown him regarding the houseboat, and the beer. I needed to find common ground, not to set us free, but to see our side of this mess. I called out for ten minutes.

Robert Dean remained silent, faced forward, his chin held low.

I, too, was losing grit faster than the chrome off a trailer hitch. For the next few minutes, I nearly passed out into a deep tiredness, where my eyelids would barely stay open. I feared warm-water hypothermia was beginning to set in, which strangled my deep breathing attempts. I drew the deepest breath I could, held it, and called out, "Who was the girl!" I called it two, three times as if they'd be the last words I'd ever speak.

"Look now," I fought to say.

Robert Dean made efforts to glance behind at the bank, checking for movement.

Water sloshed up to my neck as I studied my friend's face.

Robert Dean faced me, and his eyes said I'd done *something*, that my words were understood. "Here he come." He shifted as the sloshing grew closer.

Three Bands reached my piling, towered above, swiped the spear down clenched in his grip, then slung the gray stone tip within inches of my face.

"Do it," I said to his angered face.

Robert Dean shifted. "Uhh, Shamus?"

"What are you waiting for?" I said to the man.

In rage, he pressed the razor-sharp stone tip against my face. His nervousness reverberated down the six-foot wooden spear, shuddering the stone tip as it began to scratch my cheek. My eyes followed the length of the spear, and reaching his grip, I lifted them to his rage-filled eyes.

I'd struck a nerve, asking about the girl, but I craved to know the story behind it, and the token, so I pressed and asked again, "Who's the girl?"

A tear fell from his blacked-out eye socket, taking a tiny amount of char with it. I was getting close.

"I need to know," I said.

There was a short moment of silence as he settled. "She was my life mate."

"I saw her," I said in an empathetic tone.

His wide-open eyes turned slanted. "You lie! The *token* chooses who transitions through the portal of life!"

"Why would I lie? Look at us ... we're trapped."

"I've been told the pale skin one can be decent, but sometimes it is the opposite!"

"She spoke to me."

"You lie! She was afraid. She would never talk to you!"

"What happened to her?" I pressed.

"This question has no answer for you."

"She told me 'To him, I am sorry.'"

Another tear fell from his eye and nearly hit me on the nose. His stature loosened, and he lowered the spear. "She was my life mate," he said.

Attempting to comfort him, I said, "She's beautiful."

He nodded.

"What's this…" I lowered my chin to the token "…have to do with it? Why is it cursed?"

He answered, letting out a long breath: "It brought great pain to my people."

"What happened to her?"

"She was taken."

"How?"

"The beast took her."

"What beast?"

He pointed at my arm. "The beast from which you wear the oil."

"The gator tail," I mumbled. Then asked, "So how does that connect to the token?"

"To her, it was given."

"Who gave it to her?"

"That I do not know." He studied me, reluctant to give me the information I requested. "She arrived in the village wearing it, and from that moment on she was cursed."

"What do you mean cursed? How?"

"She was carrying my child," he said sadly, "and therefore the child became cursed."

"She was pregnant?"

The fire in his eyes dimmed and flashed bright orange. "The beast took my wife and child, and the token which drapes your chest is cursed, and you will transform."

"I'm sorry to hear that. The gator, I mean beast, killed her?"

"What's he sayin', Shamus?"

"Shhh!" I snapped at Robert Dean.

Three Bands mean-mugged Robert Dean, and continued, "Yes, the beast took her through the portal of life."

"And you think that it's because of this?" I signaled down at the token.

He pointed the spear down at my chest and the stone tip lifted it by the palm fiber. "I know as fact it's because of the token."

"How?"

His confidence rose. "The token is cursed, and he who embraces it will always lose."

"Yeah, I got that part."

"What's he sayin', Shamus?"

I turned with frustration. "He's not saying anything important. Only that his wife wore the token when a gator got her."

"A gator?"

He lowered the token. "Yes, the beast."

"Ahhh..." my friend said, making sense.

Back to Three Bands, I said, "How did you find out she was wearing the token when she died—" I corrected. "I mean taken … through the portal?"

Three Bands relaxed a bit more. He had the spear lowered by his side, using it to bear some of his weight. "The night had been cold, and judging from the taste in the air, fierce weather was near. She went out to make sure the tables were clear of the day's offerings."

"The food tables?"

He nodded.

"She left, as it was her duty to make sure the tables were wiped clean of all scraps. I asked her not. I asked her to stay or let me go with her."

"She didn't?"

"It was her duty. She told me she had to clean alone since fierce weather was near. She left me to care for our little son. She said it is her duty, and the child is too young to be out in the cold, and I should stay and tend. I waited and waited. She told me she would be gone as long as it took to get the duty done, not a flash in the sky longer, not a flash in the sky shorter.

"I waited and waited, as she told me until I couldn't wait no more. I held my son and made for the offering tables. What I found was the reason for the curse."

"What did you find? Please tell me."

"She had been taken, and all that remained was the token she wore. It had been raining many drops on the walk out, but the clouds had parted and light from the moon shone on the table where the token lay glowing as bright as a green star." He paused and faced me. "The token ... *and* blood."

"Terrible..."

His throat cleared, continued. "I followed the blood to the water's edge, where I found droppings from the beast. This is when I knew she was taken."

I shook my head.

"I and our leader met and demanded the token be vanished far from our lands."

"Over to the mangrove wall?"

"Yes, the great wall of mangroves. And then you bring it back, as it was forgotten."

"How was I supposed to know all this?"

"Knowing is not required." He began to circle me, running little waves into my neck. "The token has brought you here, not the other way."

"Why would it bring *me* here?"

"It has been returned."

"Wait!" I said as he made for the bank.

He turned back and said, "You, pale one, have learned much, and we have learned much. I will make sure your trip through the portal is well."

"Well?"

"Our leader seems to have been fond of you. Death by moon is a noble death. The sun will stay bright and will *not* turn dark." His expression straightened to stoic. "And he who embraced the token attributes death and shall take it back through the portal of life!"

He vanished through the mangrove thickets.

Robert Dean said, "I hope he went to get a knife or somethin'… to cut us loose."

"Fraid not," I said to my friend. "He did say that the sun will *not* turn dark."

"For heaven's sake. So, now we're just goin' sit here and wait for the eclipse and hope the tide doesn't come first?"

I breathed, then exhaled. "Looks like it. It's kinda hard to calculate if the tide will be in sync with the eclipse. Right now, it's low, and it may take a few more hours to reach deadly heights. The solar eclipse is forecasted to be around the same time."

"What did he say about the charm?"

"Said his wife acquired it somehow. Wore it the night a gator took her, near the food tables—blames it on the token."

"Jeezus. That *is* somethin'…"

"Said he found a blood trail to the bank near the canoes."

"Well, they should've known leavin' out big chunks of manatee meat goin' get yah in trouble."

"That's the truth, and so is the fact that this token is cursed."

"Not to be a prick, but you are kinda wearin' the thing now so…"

"Funny…"

"Really."

"What? You believing in this curse crap too?"

"I'm just sayin'… Look where we're at?"

"Yes, but that's not because the token is cursed."

"Maybe not. But you *are* wearin' it and we're about to die, Shamus!"

Our tempers triggered momentary silence. I began to fade again, an indelible drift into delirium.

*****

I must have dozed off, and when I came to, the sun shone bright in the sky, and the tide had risen. My entire lower body now remained below water, and soon my lower jaw, and soon my head.

Water also crept up to Robert Dean's neck.

We didn't have the choice to stand because they had pinned a small peg above our hands that they tied behind our backs, which stymied any attempt to stand. It occurred to me that these pilings had been used before.

"You doin' alright, bud?" Robert Dean asked.

"Just great… You?"

"Good, good," my friend said positively. "I bet he's coming back."

"I don't think so."

"You never know…"

"It'd take a phenomenon beyond our control."

We both retreated into our heads, regretting not trying to escape sooner. I wasn't fearful of the villagers, Chief, or even Three Bands. I'd put Robert Dean in danger, only for my own curiosity. It seems by nature, it's who I am.

"Remember that time when we got the Bronco stuck?" Robert Dean recollected. "Back in that rutted-out trail along a backroad canal at Port Charlotte Beach?"

"Yeah…"

"Remember how we thought we were gonna die? Because of the lack of water and no drink?"

"Yup, sure do."

"Well, we ended up *not* dying," Robert Dean said.

"Nope, we sure didn't."

"This kinda feels like that day," he continued. "We were worn clear out, I remember. We dug for what seemed like hours, then took a dunk in the canal. Cooled us off a bit, maybe helped with the heat. But it returned quick. Soon as we'd pick up diggin', we'd be right back to near death."

"Yes, but we *did* make it out."

"Eventually," my friend said.

Robert Dean's contagious drive to remain in a good place gave me the flash of optimism I needed.

I shifted, and said, "I remember us both knowing that we'd get stuck before we even tried? It was a chance we took, knowing that we couldn't possibly make it through those ruts."

"We were wet, tired, covered in dirt, grimy to the bone, and both smelled worse than that putrid ferret I dug out."

"Yeah," I said, reflecting.

"This feels like that."

Robert Dean smiled while he talked himself into positivity—a virtue to become sanguine. Our current situation was a five-star rating in hell, soul-smashing, and a murder of hope. A destruction of understanding, empathy, all receding after every wave rolled into my eyes and down my chin.

Sunlight cascaded across the open Cutoff water, twinkling atop multiple ripples. I followed a firm, straight light up to the hot sun and had to admit, the view, for quite possibly my last, wasn't bad at all. I thought about Sara. It would've been nice to see her again.

Robert Dean's head swiveled. I followed.

There it was, out of the left sky, the white moon shifting across the heavens.

"It's here!" I shouted, glancing around.

Robert Dean splashed. "What?"

"It's here. Look!" I nodded the best I could up toward the blinding sky.

"Well, I'll be dipped in shit and rolled in breadcrumbs."

"They have to see it now. The villagers *must* see it now!"

Robert Dean seemed fine, even comfy while his head cocked aside. Water lapped his jaw too, but his face was frozen into a satisfying grin. His hat sat slanted, head back, hair stubbled like a wiped-clean log forest. The piling stood two feet higher than the top of his head.

Another wave of water rolled into my chin. "Okay okay," I said to calm my excitement. "I have air, plenty of air."

Oddly, as the solar eclipse began, no animals made calls, no gull crossed the sky, nothing ruffled leaves, no mullet breached. Even the morning no-see-ums had ceased to exist.

"Hey!" I called to Robert Dean.

No answer but his head rolled to the left.

"Hey!" I spat saltwater his way.

He grunted.

"Robert Dean!"

His sublime gaze broke, and he saddened. "Oh, we're still here…?"

"Seems like it."

My friend gargled and spit as the mouth-high water splashed into his chin.

"Look!" I said toward the sky.

He looked. "I thought I was imagining it."

"Not, it's real!"

The grin returned. "Well, fry me up like a breaded cobia…"

"There it is! The solar eclipse!"

In pure astonishment, I heard a noise from the bush behind me. Rustling and the crack of mangrove branches.

"There here," I said, craning to see behind me. "They've come to spare us."

"I damn well hope so."

A train of canoes filled with men exited the mouth of the creek.

"More canoes, too," said my observant friend.

My neck cranked hard, fighting muscle cramping and saw Chief and Three Bands occupying the lead canoe. Three Bands took the rear, paddle digging into the water, acting as a rudder while Chief smoked a long-stemmed pipe, billowing circles of clouds from his mouth.

I couldn't see them in the bush, but I knew other villagers lurked behind the shadows of the mangroves, here to witness what I had decried. They were primed to believe, to subscribe to my proclamation. They had created a village that had everything required—food, shelter. All those things, discipline, conformity, they had it.

Their canoes closed in, circling at a safe distance. The villagers looked at Chief to acknowledge the strange event in the sky, that what had been prophesied by the pale one was now on full display. Had he the power to turn off the sun? If he did, then everything would change in the village—beliefs, the tainted charm, maybe even their entire way of life.

The sun was bright, like an atomic blast in the sky. Only a fool would look directly at it, so I muscled one eye closed and peeked. It was beautiful.

I peered to the chief, his canoe displacing water as Three Bands thrusted it forward.

With my hands tied, I had no way to escape, had no energy reserve to make a run for it. My life was left it in the hands of Chief. As the sky dimmed, everything began to obscure out of focus, an incorrect alignment of figures—three separating from one.

My lungs felt their final breath, and water splashed over my eyes. Suddenly, I felt the peg rip out and they lifted me while in a semi-conscious brain fog. Many of their hands clamped to my legs, my arms; pressured palms slid across my back, they hoisted me as though I'd just hit a bottom-of-the-ninth grand slam. A hand palmed, propping up my bobbling head. I saw the clouds, each a shapeshifting rolling ball of snow.

The sky went dark.

Chapter Eighteen

My **hearing** returned before my sight. I heard things before touching them. I felt movement, the slight listing of a boat adrift. "Did I go through the portal of life?" I whispered.

My friend spoke in his deep, familiar register. "What in the hell is that? Did you puke all down the railing? Dang, Shamus."

I heard it loud and clear, just like the first time I'd heard it. My eyes sprang open, and I stared up at the morning sky. I regained a little consciousness and noticed I'd slept awkwardly on the edge of the lookout atop the houseboat. "What is going on?" I mumbled.

I rolled aside and below on the deck, my friend Robert Dean, who was very much alive, was washing vomit from the side of the flat gunwale. "You missed a spot," I said automatically.

Everything felt relieved, and a proverbial scene played out, down to the spins as I rolled back onto my side.

I mumbled to myself as Robert Dean said, "You missed the water by six inches … I mean … you couldn't move six more dang inches?"

"Have you seen where I've slept?"

"And…?" he said loud and clear.

I sat up and settled cross-legged, and using my balled-up fists, I massaged my crusted eye sockets. Out toward the greasy slick Cutoff water toward the stern, where the mangrove's red roots signified low tide had arrived, a flirt of oyster was visible amid the blue-gray of dawn.

My fingers told me nothing as they held the loose token around my neck. I still had it, and from what I remembered, it had found its way back around my neck before I passed out.

I leaned to the side, ripped it off, then tossed it deep into the mangroves.

"Hey, what was in that apple pie anyway?" I said down to my friend.

"Why?" he answered with a profound blink and a grin.

"Umm, just curious…"

*****

Robert Dean and I made it through the remainder of the weekend incident-free. The fishing ended up superb, and the houseboat stayed afloat, and we stayed lit. We discussed my groundbreaking mental trip, and all the things I'd experienced in it, and most importantly, the eclipse…

He laughed at my seriousness that the village I described felt overwhelmingly real. Said that the pie "Can do that to a man" and "Like Columbus? Remember? Like when he fooled the Jamaicans with forecasting the eclipse? Guess he told those people that he could block the sun, made him a God, had the whole island at his mercy … stocked him up real good."

I asked him, "Didn't Twain write about this?"

"Who knows, but it sure as heck got 'em out of trouble."

Our trip strengthened my connection to Robert Dean. The Myakka Cutoff had helped us arrive at the end of our trip satisfied, in the exact ways we had set off to do—to let loose and charge up, mentally and emotionally, experience nature and explore new horizons. Maybe our emotions had to be drained to complete emptiness before a nurtured refiling could begin. It was, in a way, a shedding of ego, a total loss of fear and the unknowing. The ingredients for a stable mental foundation had been mixed, formed, and cured to the mite of a diamond. Our delusional near-death experience shed light on all facets of my psyche that needed, for me, the most work. Robert Dean wasn't the type to explore his emotions in public, but when he said, "This feels like that" while we were pinned to the piling, after discussing our "stuck in the sand predicament" I knew his psyche cured to new strengths, and the integrity of our friendship had reached new altitudes.

*****

When I returned to the house, and after Robert Dean had traveled back to the mountains of North Carolina, Sara Albright and I made love as though we had invented it. Her delight that I'd returned alive and willing to take our relationship to another level deepened her blush when I swept a golden lock away from her eyes.

Scupper had the most stressful time of all. Sara's parents' dog had bitten her, and she'd spent the whole weekend frightened to death, finding refuge in their bathtub.

"It should heal just fine," Sara told me while I inspected the insignificant wound across Scupper's front left paw.

"I hope so."

She said, "You'd think she'd be more of a badass, seeing as she lived on the streets for months."

I listened to Sara talk of truth while we sat on the lanai sipping cocktails. I adored her as she explained how "Chewy doesn't like to be bothered when she's eating," and how Scupper had "learned a valuable lesson." The truth was I couldn't be upset because I was so relieved to be home and alive.

The last few days seemed double to that. The visions played like I had physically and mentally lived those days. It was as though I hadn't seen Sara or Scupper in more than a week, while in reality, it had only been three days.

So, I sat and listened while she talked with her hands; used an index finger, showing the number one when she explained that Chewy had, "Never needed to share his food," and how "She ain't gonna start now." Being back felt warm. It felt right.

I picked up my cocktail, swirled the ice, and thought how deep inside I wanted the hidden village to be real. I wanted it to exist. Perhaps it did exist at one point in time and had flourished.

I giggled when she asked, "How was the eclipse?" I wanted Sara to care more about what I told her about my experience. I summoned a laugh when telling her I'd chucked the charm into the mangroves though.

I then scratched Scupper's head on my lap. Her tail wagged when her attention went out toward the basin. She rose and stuck up a wet, shiny nose, poking the door handle. I suppose she missed her friend Spinner.

I rose, and after fitting Scupper's preserver, opened the door and off she ran. I followed out the door but turned back. "You comin'?"

Sara followed me toward the houseboat lashed to the dock.

Scupper's nose remained pointed up while she barked at the edge of the boat ramp. Her movements were tentative as she pawed the water's edge.

Sara frowned. "How come she won't go in?"

"Not sure." I glanced out toward the basin and swept the surface, searching for the dolphin.

Sara suggested, "Maybe she's still freaked out from a few days ago, before you left?"

"Maybe," I replied.

Sara gazed out toward the basin and saw the same thing I did, at the same time as me. She gasped and said, "Oh! Look, Shamus!"

I inhaled. "Well, I guess now we know it's female."

Ahead of the skiff, Spinner surfaced, and beside her, a calf. The mini gray dolphin breathed in sync while nestled close to its mother.

"It's adorable, Shamus!"

I brought Sara into my arms, squeezed her tight, and said, "Don't go getting any ideas."

The End

You can contact David Earth here:
earthtodavid101@gmail.com

If you leave a supporting review,
it would be much appreciated.